Between Enzo & the Universe

Chase Connor

The Lion Fish Press

Chase Connor Books

The Lion Fish Press

www.chaseconnor.com

www.thelionfishpress.com

Book Cover Designed By: Allen T. St. Clair, ©2019 Chase Connor

CHASE CONNOR BOOKS are published by

The Lion Fish Press
539 W. Commerce St #227
Dallas, TX 75208

AUTHORS' NOTE:
This is a work of fiction. Names, characters, places, and incidents either are the product of the authors' imagination or are used fictitiously, and any resemblance to actual persons, living or dead, business establishments, events, or locales is entirely coincidental. None of this is real.
ENZO takes place in a fictionalized version of Montreal, Québec, Canada. Some geographical details and information have been changed to work better with the story. This is all fiction.

Ebook ISBN 978-1-951860-00-4
Paperback ISBN 978-1-951860-02-8
Hardback ISBN 978-1-951860-01-1

As always:

To my beta-readers and "feedback crew": I am so glad you are all here. And I am so glad you are all so blunt with me—even if I do what I want most of the time.

To all of the readers: It has been quite a journey. I've loved every second of it. Let's get to the end together, shall we?

Also by Chase Connor

Just a Dumb Surfer Dude: A Gay Coming-of-Age Tale
Just a Dumb Surfer Dude 2: For the Love of Logan
Just a Dumb Surfer Dude 3: Summer Hearts
Gavin's Big Gay Checklist
A Surplus of Light
The Guy Gets Teddy
GINJUH
A Tremendous Amount of Normal
The Gravity of Nothing

A Point Worth LGBTQ Paranormal Romances

Jacob Michaels Is Tired (Book 1)
Jacob Michaels Is Not Crazy (Book 2)
Jacob Michaels Is Not Jacob Michaels (Book 3)
Jacob Michaels Is Not Here (Book 4)
Jacob Michaels Is Trouble (Book 5)
CARNAVAL (A Point Worth LGBTQ Paranormal Romance Story)
Jacob Michaels Is Dead (Book 6)

Erotica

Bully

Audiobooks

A Surplus of Light (narrated by Brian Lore Evans)

For my best friend.
Within my heart lives a love no romance could ever fathom.

Between Enzo & the Universe

Chapters

The Coat Made of Sugar and Blue Clouds

Sugar was what my brother's coat always smelled like because his favorite activity was going to the bakery to watch the donuts being fried in the giant vats of grease and then being glazed while they were still piping hot. The bakers used long sticks—almost like giant chopsticks—to flip the puffed-up circles of dough when one side had been fried through. After both sides of the donuts were fried thoroughly, they were systematically and uniformly flipped onto a draining rack and immediately smothered in a sugary waterfall of nearly translucent liquid that would eventually dry to a shiny white. The process of watching the bakers work, systematically frying, flipping, removing, and icing was what made the bakery a magical place for my brother. Watching the donuts being fried was not a quick process, so the smell of warm sugar that permeated the relatively small shop's interior had ample opportunity to affix itself to his coat. His coat getting a dose of the sugary scent was all that we usually left the donut shop with since I often could not afford to buy any actual donuts. The show was free, so the budget was forgiving of each viewing. What little money I had in my pocket was often used for bus fare to and from the shop. Sometimes, if it was a good

1

day for my brother, we would walk to the shop, and I would use half of the money to take us home from the shop. I would use the other half for a few donuts for him. He would eat them on the bus ride home. Under normal circumstances, we could have walked the 8 kilometers comprising the round trip from our apartment to the shop, and used all of the money for an entire box of donuts. Still, even one way was often too much for him.

My brother, Noe, never complained about walking since he knew that donuts would be his reward, but I had to be cognizant of whether or not any given day was a good day or bad day. Regularly, I was correct in determining if Noe could make it to the shop on foot or not, whether or not we were having a good or bad day, so we rarely encountered any difficulty. Walks to the donut shop were the best days. Days of exercise and warm sun on our faces or blustery wind at our backs, and warm sugary icing that always ended up smeared across his chin and cheeks as he sat, content and presenting his version of a smile, on the bus ride home. Those days he didn't mind when I used a napkin and the bottle of water I always carried on our trip to wash his face while he sat there in his sugary, splendid stupor. The flick of his eyes to glance at my face, the half-smile he gave when he was happy and full of fried dough, as I gently cleaned him off and strangers watched on with bewilderment, made me happy. It didn't always, as

2

strangers on a bus could often make things uncomfortable for Noe and me, but that was rare since most people on a bus in the early morning just want to get home or to work without unnecessary human contact.

Noe was always proud of his bright blue puffy coat, believing that it made him look like a cloud, even though clouds are white. There was no point in reminding him of this because Noe wasn't stupid, he just saw things differently than others. Whether we walked to the shop or rode the bus, he was proud to be bundled tightly in his coat when it was cold. He would walk proudly in his coat made of clouds the color of the sky, and I would walk proudly alongside him, pulling my sweater tightly around myself, making do with what I had.

It hadn't always been like that, one brother in a sufficient coat and the other hoping that the budget would soon allow for the purchase of a coat for himself. For many years, none of us had gone without coats, nor had we had to endure walks in the snow with nothing more than a bulky sweater to chase away the icy wind. We hadn't eaten boxed pasta, boiled and served with only butter as a sauce for dinner five nights a week. When butter was a luxury the budget allowed us to purchase. Times had not always dictated that we choose between Noe's inhalers and a winter coat for the oldest of us kids. We hadn't always found ourselves choosing between having a sofa and paying rent, or sitting on the floor and having a warm place to call home. It wasn't common in our past for me to have to wash clothes in our sink and dry them on a rack in the corner of our nearly barren living room. Money and time fluctuate with the health and abilities of the members of a family, though.

October in the city is often cool during the day, bordering on bitter at night, so I was glad to have that warm sugary smell wrapped around me as I walked Saint Urbain Street. The cloying sweetness of the sugar had been fading from the coat over time, though I had not washed it in the two months that it had belonged to me. Washing the coat was out of the question until the smell had dissipated completely, not just because I had no washing machine or money to visit a laverie, but because I did not want to forget the smell. There had always been the option of walking to the bakery on a morning when I had nothing to do, which was more often than not, but, like a laverie, the bakery seemed a luxury that I could not afford.

While the coat kept me mostly warm, the thin canvas of the sneakers I had found in a thrift shop worked to counteract that warmth. Luckily, I had warm winter socks, one luxury I did not have to do without, though they had been darned many times, so the thin canvas was not as awful as it could have been. Of course, wool-lined boots would have been preferable to sneakers as we approached the coldest months of the year in the city, but that was a dream I didn't bother dreaming. My head stayed down in an attempt to keep my ears inside the collar of the coat, though it was an impossible task to complete gracefully while walking down a busy city street. When I accidentally bumped into the man, obviously better prepared in the clothing department than I, it was motivation to give up my attempt at keeping my ears warm.

"*Désolé, monsieur.*"

I had responded automatically to gloss over my clumsiness. The man barely glanced at me before he spat.

"*Putain étrangers.*"

I didn't bother saying anything further since the man had accurately pegged me as non-Canadian by birth. Many Québécois easily singled me out as being foreign by birth, though I was never able to determine if this was the slight differences in the pronunciations in our shared language, or maybe it was my eyes. Possibly a combination of the two informed the decision on their part, but being meek and often terrified of the people in my foreign home, I didn't have the skills to figure out how to ask this of someone. Not that I knew of many people who would be willing to answer such a question. When people are approached with questions about why many people in their homeland are biased against foreigners, one is often met with, at the very least, resistance.

Expletives spat at the ground, and insults, if not outright aggression and violence, are not out of the question.

So, I allowed myself to be a *fucking foreigner.* At least I had said "sorry" for my clumsiness, so I was a *polite fucking foreigner.*

ESL classes—English as a Second Language—can be expensive. In Québec, the official language could be considered French, thanks to The Official Language Act of 1974. *French Loi sur la langue officielle*—or *Loi sur la langue officielle française*, depending upon whom is speaking. It was replaced by the Charter of the French Language in 1977. However, due to objections about the act, also known as *Bill 22*, and to the charter, English is also an official language. So, French is taught as a primary language in schools from Grade 1 upwards, with English as a second language. Because of this, Québécois are expected to know and use both languages as becomes appropriate; thus, ESL classes are often seen as redundant or a waste of time. ESL classes for people whom English is actually their third language is even more uncommon. Many who may disagree that ESL classes, or English language classes in general, are affordable and immersive have the privilege of having hundreds of dollars to spend for things besides absolute necessities.

My budget afforded very little besides the roof over my head, the clothes on my back (though the articles I possessed were few), and the meager meals I managed zero to three times a day, depending upon the day. Language classes were beyond my reach, so finding a way to pay for them got increasingly creative on my part. In fact, actual, certified ESL classes were so expensive that my creativity was not enough, which was why I took English classes in a room above a dumpling restaurant in the Red-Light District. While this may not seem ideal, and I would be the first to admit that the classes were not of the quality one would expect from a language class a person actually paid money to attend, it was not far from Notre-Dame Basilica, which I enjoyed walking past at least once a day if I could manage it. From there, I could walk to a much smaller chapel to do my daily prayers, though I was steadfastly against visiting the confessional unless I had experienced a particularly trying day. Confession hours did not fit within my schedule anyway, so I felt justified in ignoring that particular custom of my religion.

My prayers never changed, though they rarely strayed into traditional Catholic prayer, instead taking the form of a personal conversation with my Lord and Savior, though I often felt he chose not to listen. God had bigger problems than the dilemmas of Enzo, so I did not take it personally when I rose from the kneeler or stone floor after prayer each time. My prayers became predetermined and reiterative after going to church following a visit to see my mother in the hospital one evening and learning a lesson about prayer the hard way. As the sun had sunk past the horizon that evening, the stained glass in the few windows of the chapel turning blue, red, and purple, I had asked for help with our financial hardships.

PleaseGodgivemeawaytogetmoremoneyformyfamily.

The thought entered my brain like a tsunami before I could stop myself, and I immediately felt guilty, as though I had brought shame upon myself in my sinful ways there in the chapel.

As I had left the church, walking in the near darkness along the street, a man standing in the alcove of a closed shop had suggested that certain activities would lead to money in my pocket. As though Satan, instead of God, had heard my prayers. "You only have to stand there," he had explained quickly as a follow-up.

Tapette!

He had screamed after me when I hurried away, my head lowered in panic. Unsure if I spoke French, apparently, he screamed at me once again in English in that increasing distance between us.

Faggot!

I had never asked for material things again.

And my prayers became much more refined.

Simple.

Focused.

In the moments following that incident, I couldn't help but feel that my meager clothing and meek manner, as well as my selfish prayers, had caused the problem. Obviously, I looked like a homeless teenager—hungry, downtrodden, willing to do anything—even allow a strange man to put his mouth on me—for something as simple as a hot meal or a warm coat. I cursed myself for having a problem that I did not have money to fix. I cursed myself further for considering whether or not I could force myself do such a thing with a stranger for my family if necessary, though circumstances changed before I had to definitively face that question.

Monsieur Paquette wasn't a bad teacher, all things considered. Let me rephrase. Mr. Paquette was a perfectly serviceable teacher. He did teach his ESL class over a dumpling restaurant in the Red-Light District, but he spoke English very well, especially for a fellow immigrant. At least, it sounded as though he spoke it well, and my fellow students seemed quite pleased with the way he spoke it. Since they all spoke English well, I had to assume that my fellow students were a good barometer for the quality of the class. It never occurred to me at the time that my fellow students were probably attending an ESL class in the small room over a dumpling restaurant because, like me, they had no other choice. Their barometers were perhaps not the best instruments by which to judge the weather.

Entering the restaurant, the cooks and waitstaff in the often-desolate interior, looked up, hopeful at first, then utterly disappointed. I waved awkwardly and bounded up the stairs at the side of the heavenly warm room that was always thick with sticky, humid air permeated with the smell of garlic and onion and exotic spices, to attend my class. Mr. Paquette had already begun, all of my fellow students in uncomfortable folding chairs in a half-circle around him as he pointed and poked at a dry erase board full of words that still sometimes looked like nonsense to me. Understanding English as spoken, compared to written, was much easier for me then. A stern look met me as Mr. Paquette paused only briefly, then a bony finger turned into a half-hook and jabbed in the direction of the open seat on his left. Lowering my head in apology, I quickly took off my coat, hung it on the only free hook by the door, and scurried to the seat. Mr. Paquette continued his lesson, firing off words in French and pointing at a student to translate it into English, then use it in a full sentence *en Anglais, s'il vous plait.*

It was not lost on me that most, if not all, of my fellow students were given much more difficult words than I, though I tried not to be embarrassed. None of my fellow students ever said anything, but there were often exchanged glances and snickers if I struggled with the most basic of English words. It was not that I did not speak English well, I just did not speak

10

it well enough and fast enough, so my confidence in speaking it around my fellow students caused me to fuck up sometimes. That's what I thought to myself often, though, if asked to explain by Mr. Paquette, I would say, in my slow, measured English: *"I struggle to think quickly enough to say the words in the right sequence to be correct."*

This, too, would cause glances to be exchanged and snickers to be…*snicked?*

"Hello, Enzo." Mr. Paquette asked suddenly after making his way down his row of students. "How are you doing this evening?"

"I am doing good, Mr. Paquette."

"You are well." He corrected me, his eyes peering at me over the glasses I was certain served only a theatrical purpose. "We do good through actions, and we are feeling well."

"Bien sûr, Monsieur Paquette."

He sighed.

Snickers.

Holding back from cringing, I cleared my throat.

"Of course, Mr. Paquette. Thank you. I am sorry."

"We are not sorry in this class." He went to the board to start another lesson. "We just try harder each time."

Instead of responding, I sank back into my chair, tucked my knees in and hunched my back, trying to make my tall, lanky frame disappear in the half-circle of my fellow students. For the remaining fifty minutes, for I had missed the first ten, I held my body in, making it as compact and as invisible as possible. By the time that Mr. Paquette dismissed us, urging us to read an American or British classic novel in the following week, my joints hurt, and my neck felt as though it was on fire. My fellow students thanked Mr. Paquette, *en Anglais*, of course, and exited class in a lively, raucous group, speaking of plans to go have drinks. None of them turned to offer an invitation as they passed. My knees popped as I rose from the folding chair, and Mr. Paquette was methodically wiping the board clean. The French language class for immigrants would be conducted the following night, so Mr. Paquette liked to be prepared.

"Monsieur Paquette?" I always approached him after class, though I knew he was as anxious to be somewhere else as my fellow students were. "Devrais-je nettoyer maintenant?"

"Enzo." Mr. Paquette turned to me, his eyes already gazing over the tops of his glasses. "If you do not practice speaking English, you will not get better at speaking English. Yes?"

"I speak English fine."

"Your English is lazy and slow." His looks were always stern, but his eyes radiated warmth. Usually, only when speaking with me. And only when we were alone. With everyone else, he was direct and cold, though he could feign friendliness just fine if a student required it. "You come to my classes and only interact when forced. Enzo, have you thought of returning to France? There is nothing keeping you here now."

My bottom lip may have jutted out as I looked away, doing anything I could to keep my eyes turned away from his. Mr. Paquette, having realized what he had said, cleared his throat, and tried once more.

"You are free to make choices that are best for you." He said. "You do not need to consider anyone else now. Have you considered that Québec does not feel like home to you?"

Finally, I risked a glance in his direction.

"I have no one left in Mantes." I made sure to speak in English, though I took my time with my words. "It is just me."

"Exactly." His eyes seemed to light from within. "You are free of all constraint. You could go to Paris or Nantes! Marseilles or Monaco! Think of the possibilities, Enzo. The whole world is yours to claim if you were to just take a risk."

Maybe you plan to fund this travel, Monsieur Paquette?

"Yes," I said slowly. "Yes, sir. Thank you."

He sighed, his body slumping. Obviously, my eyes had told a tale.

"You look hungry, Enzo."

"Would you like me to sweep the floors?" I asked, ignoring his observation. "Should I put the chairs away tonight or tomorrow night?"

Mr. Paquette reached into the back pocket of his trousers as I asked a second time about my cleaning duties, though in English this time—my creative method for paying to attend ESL classes. It was an arrangement Mr. Paquette and I had agreed upon merely a day before the class began.

"Enzo." He glanced up from his wallet momentarily. "I want you to go get something to eat. The room is clean enough for class tomorrow. You can clean tomorrow night."

"Mrs. Bishop will expect me at her house to clean tomorrow," I said. "Is it sufficient to clean the room after that?"

"It's *acceptable* for you to clean after that." He actually smiled as he pulled a bill out of his wallet and presented it to me. "Go eat. Please."

I didn't dare let my eyes turn to the money held out to me.

As is often the case, my stomach groaned desperately, betraying my fixed expression.

Mr. Paquette pretended to not hear while I pretended to not feel it.

"Charity was not offered when it was most useful," I said sharply, my English improving considerably for a moment. "I do not need it now."

"Enzo." Mr. Paquette gestured sternly with the money. "This is not charity, and now is not those times. Please get something to eat. It would mean a great deal to me."

My eyes flicked to his hand.

Twenty dollars. Mentally I calculated how many dumplings twenty dollars would buy in the restaurant below. I could eat until I was sick and torpid. Saliva pooled at the back of my mouth as I thought of the warm soup and crunchy wontons, the steaming, doughy dumplings, a cup of herbal tea, and maybe even a moon cake. Or two. The sun was beginning its journey to meet the Western horizon, and I did not have to linger behind in class to clean. If I walked to the Autumn festival that was just beginning in the city center, I would be able to buy even more food. The street vendors and food carts sold heaping plates of food for barely any money. I could eat until my stomach was extended and still afford food to take home and put in the refrigerator for the following days. Cautiously, I reached out to take the money from Mr. Paquette.

"Oh." His hand retracted and went back to his wallet.

Of course. This was all a game. How stupid of me.

"Here, Enzo." His hand returned, another bill in his hand this time. "As you know, we will not have class next week, but I would still like the room cleaned as usual. Since I will not be able to teach, you cannot be expected to clean for free."

Biting the inner part of my bottom lip, willing my eyes to not betray me, I reached out and took the forty dollars from his hand. It was as if my hand moved in slow motion, afraid to startle him, as though that would convince him to take the money back. But the money finally found its way into my front hip pocket.

"It will be spot free when you return to class, Mr. Paquette."

It was the only response I could conjure.

"*Spotless.*" He smiled. "Now, go. Get something to eat, Enzo. Have a drink like your peers."

They are not my peers.

"I do not drink, sir."

His brow rose, appraising me.

"Maybe just this once?" He finally responded.

I smiled. Again, unable to conjure a better response. Mr. Paquette patted my shoulder firmly, the way that men like to do to other men as a sign of affection that is not too familiar so as not to be misconstrued. Mr. Paquette turned back to the board to continue his task of clearing away his lessons, and I made my way to the exit, already calculating how many dishes of food I could buy. The coat made of sugar and blue clouds had disappeared from the hook by the door. There was no point in looking to see if it had been misplaced. I descended the stairs without hesitation, knowing that I would never see my brother's coat again.

I wanted to be angry.

When I rushed through the restaurant at the bottom of the stairs and burst out onto the sidewalk, anger was not what spilled forth. I rounded the corner of the restaurant, the bitter wind biting through my sweater, and dropped to my knees at the side of the building, my forehead falling against the cold, rough wall. My tears became wet, black circles on the gray stone.

Fuck.

Five is Better Than Four

My parents had prepared me for the day that my brother joined our family. The setting for the conversation had not been ideal, but I had not been allowed to leave the hospital from my most recent stay at that point. Actually, the first conversation about our family becoming bigger began when I wasn't in the hospital. It had begun as a low rumble of statements. About how so many children with "special circumstances" needed a family to welcome and love them. To treat them as one of their own. So, it was no surprise to me, as I laid in the hospital bed with half of my head shaved and a tube going into my arm, my eyes with black half-moons underneath them, that my parents made the announcement that I was getting a new brother. I was still young then, barely a double-digit age, when my parents, one on either side of my hospital bed, each reached up to lay a hand on one of my knees. Dad, as he always did, squeezed my knee and jostled me, which always made me giggle but frightened my mother. She didn't understand boys like my father and I did. This was our secret language, knowing what our bodies could endure, even at their weakest. Guys can admit their fragilities, but they hate to abide them. They hate it more when other guys do.

Noe was his name. A boy from a foreign land—though, luckily, one where French was a common language—who had been abandoned by his parents, though the reason why wasn't provided to me at that age. I would have to wait five years before my parents sat me down to explain that some parents do not want children who are different. Of course, by then, I had already figured things out for myself, though it was nice to feel that I was a *man*—capable of being allowed into my parents' confidence. My new brother, as was relayed to me when his arrival was imminent, would *be different* from me. He wouldn't exactly look like he was my brother, and he might not treat me like I was his brother upon his arrival. My parents explained that this did not make him any less my brother or any less a member of our family. We were going to accept him, have patience with him, and love him as if he had been with us since birth.

I was so excited.

If Noe arrived with two heads, I would still have a brother.

And then I would have two different faces with whom to talk to about brotherly things.

Embarrassingly, I began to wonder if it was pointless to pray for such a thing.

Receiving two brothers when you only expected one would be glorious.

Having more children had not been possible for my parents after I was born, and even if it had been, they had been inspired by my own medical issues to help other children with "special circumstances." Because of this, I lived believing that I would never have a brother or sister to tease and torment, to love and protect, to take under my wing and guide. I wouldn't have a brother or sister who would look up at me adoringly and who I could introduce to my friends with my chest puffed out with pride, though, of course, I would pretend that they were the greatest annoyance of my life. All of the kids in my school—we were still in France then—seemed to have at least one sibling, yet I had none. Getting a brother, knowing that all that was left to do was to wait for him to arrive, was like Christmas morning when I would first roll over in bed and see the light trying to peek through the curtains. Or *Réveillon* and Midnight Mass the night before. It was as if I had put my shoes by the fireplace, and I was waiting to wake up and find my brother as my gift.

Upon Noe's arrival, he was nothing I had expected. Not because his skin was many shades darker than mine or my parents'. Noe was delivered to our home by a very stern and orderly woman in a suit nearly one full size larger than necessary. She kept glaring at me as I held onto my father's hand with both of mine and grinned at my new brother, hoping he would look up and smile back. Maybe he would look up and smile back, suggest we go play. I knew that since he was barely half my age, he might not like to do the same things as me, but anything would be fine by me. As long as I got to play with my new brother. He never looked up and smiled. He didn't speak. He did not acknowledge that he was aware of our family's existence.

Noe didn't like to look people in the eyes. He didn't like for people to touch him, even if by accident. He only spoke when absolutely necessary, and his way of saying things required more understanding and deciphering, and he rarely wanted to actively participate in play. He could stare at the neighbor's dog playing in the yard for hours on end. He refused to eat foods with blended textures. He liked one pair of shoes and one shirt, wanting to wear them every day, which led to many challenges each morning. He had a lung disease, that I eventually learned was chronic obstructive pulmonary disease, which was quite rare in such a young person, though a deficiency of some kind of protein had led to this diagnosis. In addition to that, his additional diagnosis of asthma required the use of an inhaler multiple times in a day. He tired quickly, and most exercise, even walking sometimes, proved difficult for him.

The challenges thrilled me. Because Noe was quiet and peaceful. He did not run through the house, screaming. He didn't take my things. He didn't hit me or call me names. He was quite peaceful, especially compared to the stories my friends told about their siblings. Noe was happy to watch me play while I told him all about my toys and books without interrupting me. He loved to listen to me talk, which made me feel very important at that age since no one had felt that what I had to say was worth hearing before then. And at least the shirt and shoes he liked to wear were actually pretty cool. He loved the color blue and eventually grew to tolerate me accidentally brushing against him or touching him while we spent time together, sitting on my bedroom floor, playing with my toys. As time passed, when we walked along the street, he would let me hold onto his forearm so that I knew he was safe and wouldn't accidentally step in front of a motorist or bicyclist. The "hiss" of his inhaler didn't bother me when he used it and actually sounded cool like a special effects noise from a science fiction movie. I loved the challenges presented in helping to care for my brother, in protecting him from a world that was much too harsh for him.

He would smile awkwardly when I managed to get him to walk next door to visit the neighbor's dog—a Spaniel mix of some kind with splotches of brown and white and big floppy ears with fur cascading from them that looked like fringe. I would always have to hold the dog to be certain that it would not jump on Noe as I petted its fur and scratched its ears. Somehow, the dog seemed to understand the reason for me having to hold it still in order for it to receive affection from me, for it was almost reverent around my brother. Noe would clasp his hands and watch with intense concentration as I would pet the dog. I knew that my brother desperately wanted to pet the dog as well, but all of that fur, at all times both coarse and silky, would not be tolerable for him. I would just hold and pet the dog and tell Noe how much the dog was happy that he had come to visit him. We visited the dog often when the weather permitted. Until the neighbor asked my parents that they not let Noe into his yard anymore.

The neighbor said that I was still welcome.

I never went back into that yard.

But I felt sorry for the dog.

How much love could a person provide for their pet when they could not even find it in their heart to be indifferent, at the very least, to a young child?

A year after Noe joined our household, my grandfather died, and my grandmother came from Paris to live with us. So, four became five. And Noe had a new favorite person. My grandmother had visited many times in the year previous, and Noe had shown interest in this older woman with the dark, fluffy cotton-candy hair that had not been faded by time. He loved the sparkle of the rings on her fingers and the way her earrings swung as she spoke in her perpetually enthusiastic way. He loved the peppermints that she kept in her handbag and the way she would make sure her hand didn't touch his whenever she gave him one. My grandmother became only the second person Noe would allow to touch him in any way. In fact, until he became too old, thus too heavy, he eventually came to enjoy sitting in her lap to watch the television with her. He didn't even care which show she chose to watch. Her lap was one of the very few safe spaces the noisy, boisterous world provided for Noe.

Both my favorite and worst memory of having a new brother was the day that I had been able to introduce Noe to my friends from school. They had followed me home one day so that they could see my new brother. I suppose I had misled them in how excitedly I had talked about having a new brother and how *trop cool* he was.

That day was when I found out what "retard" meant in both French and English, though my English was very poor then.

I also learned a derogatory term for people with skin the color of Noe's, though I have never been able to say or write the word since without rage overtaking me.

Remembering that word coming from the mouths of my three friends in turn still makes my hands shake and my eyes well with tears, a systematic preparation for an explosion of emotion of some kind, though I never know if it will be violence or weeping.

That was also the day that I had my first real fight.

And I decided that the only friend I needed was my brother. Because no one needs friends who use such words.

Red is the Color of Atonement

The side of the building which housed the dumpling restaurant and my ESL classes was unforgiving, of both my fists and my tears. Truth be told, I had never been much of one for crying. Crying had been unsettling to Noe and, eventually, to my sister. My parents were not overly emotional people, either, so over time, I had trained myself to express sadness in a different way. As I knelt along the wall of the restaurant, my forehead against the frigid stone, the sides of my fists pounding against an unmovable and undefeatable enemy, I did not cry. I sobbed. Gasping, wail-like sobs, accompanied by the fattest tears I'd ever cried, escaped my throat. Surely, if an officer with the SPVM had happened by, I would have been taken away. Possibly to jail, but most likely to a hospital, such was my display of grief.

Over a coat.

My gasping and wailing were not for the coat, though. They were for my brother. His coat had been the last thing that remained of him. It was the last material thing I had to remind me of my family. Maybe, if I had been able to wear the coat until the warm sugar smell had completely faded, I wouldn't have been as upset at someone having stolen the coat. They had probably done it simply to be cruel. Because they could. Telling my fellow students about my brother and why I *needed* that coat and the smell of sugar would not have swayed them from enacting such a cruelty. Cruel people do not have mercy simply because their target is barely hanging on by the skin of their teeth. They do not care why a coat is important to you. They do not care when you had your last meal. They do not care that you cannot get approved for enough public assistance to fully pay for the medications your brother needs. They do not care that a roof over your head and a coat on your back are the only shelter you have from the world. Cruelty never considers these things.

The sobs tapered off, and I ceased pounding the meaty parts of my fists against the wall because I knew I was already going to end up with bruises. Holding a broom or a cloth to clean the following day was going to be torture. I did not want to make it worse. Snorting and sniffling, I rose from my knees, bracing myself against the wall with my hands. My vision was blurry, and I knew that my eyes were reddened and puffy because the bitter wind stung as it slapped against the apples of my cheeks. I had forty dollars. I could fix this problem. Maybe I would never see my brother's coat again, nor smell the memories it contained, but I could fix the immediate problem. I pulled the cuff of my sweater sleeve over the back of my hand and used it to wipe my eyes and then under my nose, hoping that I did not look homeless. It would be difficult to fix my problem if I looked as though I had been sleeping in an alleyway or a church pew at night.

Trained for the task, my legs began to move without me even considering where I was going, turning me towards the city center. My feet moved, my toes cold and stiff within my canvas shoes, and I huddled within my sweater as I walked. I always walked. Walking is what kept me from staying still too long. Moving is what propels you forward, keeps you from sinking, so I always made sure that I was moving when I was awake. People I passed on the street mostly shot glances in my direction, though a few offered up varieties of "Hello" in both English and French. I did my best to return their greetings, or at least nod as I passed, but my heart was not in the gestures. I wanted to tell everyone to "fuck off," though I knew that was not what I truly wanted. In my heart of hearts, I wanted to plead with someone:

Please show me kindness. Pleasepleasepleasepleaseplease.

And in doing so, I would not be treated like a crazy person. That people would not back away in fear or agitation, but instead, realize that another human being needed someone—anyone—to let them know that they were not as alone as they felt. Desperately, I sought any indication in the faces of the people I passed that kindness might be within their capabilities. The looks of concern and worry at walking by me in my canvas shoes and old sweater and torn jeans painted most of the faces I passed. Even the ones that offered up a greeting. So, I kept my thoughts to myself, did not let anyone know that I was one act of cruelty away from deciding to stay still. I would stop moving, stop propelling myself always forward, and just allow what was to come.

The thought was almost comforting. I could stand there in the street and listen to the people scream *"tapette"* or *"faggot"* or *"putain étrangers"* or any other insult. At least I would not be moving, wondering if my next step would be the one where the ground crumbled beneath my feet.

In the city center, the autumn festival was celebrated every year, usually during the first full week of October. Vendors of varying sorts congested the walkways and squares with food carts and temporary tents to sell their wares. The festival was to celebrate autumn, naturally, and the end of harvest, but over the years, as had been relayed to me, it had turned into one big flea market, essentially. There was some culture in the event, but mostly it was for tourists looking for cheap ethnic and regional foods or to buy a souvenir to take home when they left. Cheap clothing could also be purchased, from graphic t-shirts and sweaters emblazoned with "CANADA" in gigantic letters, to cheap knock-off shoes, and even coats. The coats were what I was most interested in—besides the food—once I reached the perimeter of the festival's boundaries.

Going to an actual clothing store to purchase an appropriate winter coat would take all of my forty dollars—if that was even enough. But I could surely find a cheap winter coat at the festival and still maybe have half of my money left to buy enough food to make myself sick.

As I walked through the street, finally finding tents and stalls and food carts scattered about, bright twinkling lights strung overhead and children running through the streets with glow sticks and fiber-optic wands, my cheeks and eyes did not feel as swollen and raw. Having no idea where to begin, as I had never really spent much time at the autumn festival in the handful of years that I had lived in the city after emigrating from France. So, I walked. And I turned. I peered down every alleyway and street, read signs, and watched the people around me, seeing if I could figure out which area of the festival the people seemed to think was best. Passing the food carts with the food warmers, grills, and fryers permeating the air with steam heat, made my lack of an appropriate coat not as apparent to me. My stomach grumbled and complained with each food cart or stand I passed, especially when the vendors would scream out the names of the foods they had prepared, but I refused to relent to my stomach until I had found a coat.

I did not want to fill my stomach and then find that I had insufficient funds for a coat.

Warm sugar wafted through the air, catching my nose, threatening to make my eyes water again. As I turned to seek out the smell, I found a fried dough vendor a few meters away, selling what were essentially round donuts filled with jam and covered with confectioner's sugar. I watched at a distance as one of the workers used a sieve to sift the sugar, like a cloud of fairy dust, over the balls of light dough that were still hot from the vat of grease in which they'd been fried. My stomach threatened so loudly to revolt that I was nearly compelled to give up on my search for a coat. A flash of red caught my eye, and glancing to the left of the food vendor, I saw a tent full of clothes. Hung from one of the columns holding the awning aloft was a bright red Cocoon coat.

Surely, this coat is for women.

It looks like wool.

I bet it smells like the sugar from the food tent.

As I approached the tent, my hand anxiously slipping into my front hip pocket so that my frozen fingers could feel for the two bills given to me by Mr. Paquette, I realized that the coat was indeed intended for women. It was slightly tapered through the waist and hips, though I knew that would not be a problem for me. Getting closer, I could tell that it was probably not wool, but some synthetic material that was

32

passable for wool. If you squinted your eyes tightly enough. My fingers found the sleeve of the coat and felt of the material. While it looked as though it would feel scratchy against my skin, its appearance belied its softness.

Red is a pretty color.

But this is for women.

I reached out and flipped over the price tag that was hung from the sleeve with a cord.

Twenty dollars.

It feels warm, and it is exactly half of the money you have, as you wished.

Beggars cannot be choosers, and I should not have lost Noe's coat anyway.

This coat will be my atonement.

I brought the sleeve to my nose and inhaled.

Warm sugar.

Sighing to myself, wanting to be unhappy with finding a warm coat that would fit that would not take all of my unearned dollars, I chose to be happy. Even if it might be intended for women, no one would know that when I wore it. It was inexpensive—obviously shoddily made—though it would last through the winter. My intention, as my fingers dropped away, letting the price tag fall back into place, was to get the attention of the vendor to ask to purchase the coat. However, loud English, something that always caught my attention, and the flash of more red, drew me away from the coat and the tent.

At the vendor selling the jam-filled donuts next to the clothing tent, one of the workers was having an animated discussion with a man standing on the other side of the counter. My head tilted to the side as I took in the tall—though not quite as tall as me—man, with the shock of red hair atop his head. Long and wavy on top, brushed towards the back of his head, and much shorter on the sides, it was a very stylish haircut. His skin was pale, a stark contrast to the dark black of the heavy wool peacoat he wore, and the gray scarf wrapped loosely around his neck. He looked like something out of a fashion magazine—one which I would never be able to afford. He spoke English perfectly, though loudly.

American.

I found myself smiling.

Americans, though sometimes a bit much at once, were friendly.

I loved the way they always smiled with their teeth showing.

I loved their attempts to speak French when asking for directions. They butchered my native tongue in the most glorious ways.

When we had lived in France, many of my fellow countrymen and women barely hid their annoyance with *touristes*—especially Americans. But I had always found their boisterousness and friendliness exciting and refreshing—a stark contrast to the *blasé* and *perpétuellement irrité* disposition of everyone else.

America had always seemed so exotic to me, though I knew embarrassingly little about it that was probably actually true. All I knew about America I had learned from shows I had seen on television or movies I had seen in the cinema. It seemed like a theme park. One I would have given anything to attend for even a single day. It was garish and loud and rude and boisterous and bright. Everything about it appalled me. I wanted so desperately to visit one day.

"How much?" The American asked the vendor.

The vendor appraised the man, sizing him up. Obviously, he had figured out, just as I had, that the man was not Québécois.

"Quoi?" The vendor held his hands up, making me frown.

He spoke English. He was giving the man a hard time. Just because he could.

"Money?" The man asked as he reached for his pocket, finally extracting his wallet to wave at the vendor. "How much?"

"Cinq dollars pour toi, mec." The vendor replied, causing my frown to deepen at his extremely informal, thus rude, response to a stranger.

The man with the stylish red hair's eyes seemed to scan the air around him, his brain trying to understand what this man said to him. A few moments later, a smile bloomed on his face, obviously figuring out which number "cinq" was in English. He began to open his wallet, a wicked grin overtaking the vendor's face as he watched the man reach for a bill. Frowning to myself, and going against what was typical of my behavior, I found my feet move into action, closing the few meters distance between myself and the man with the red hair.

Without thinking, I placed a hand over his wallet, shoving it down. "*Non.*" I turned to the vendor without even looking at the American in the eyes first and began speaking in rapid French. "*A basket of these costs two dollars at most. You are not going to charge him five dollars and give him just one of your shitty donuts in exchange.*"

"*Shitty?*" The vendor's chest puffed out, and his cheeks turned red as he replied in French. "*You obviously have not had them.*"

"*For five dollars I couldn't afford to, sir.*" I snapped back in French.

Out of the corner of my eye, I could see the American examining me, wondering what was going on, especially since a few people nearby had taken notice of my arguing with the vendor.

"And he speaks English just as we do," I said in my slow, measured, though heavily accented, English. "Do not pretend you do not know what he is asking so that you can screw him over with your overpriced food."

The American man let out a barking, shocked laugh as the vendor's face grew redder.

"You little piece of—" The vendor began, glowering at me, which made me back up marginally.

I can be bold but not so bold as to welcome a physical fight over street food.

"Hey!" The American barked, his brow furrowing. "There's no reason to argue. Or be rude, sir."

He was speaking to the vendor. Not me. The vendor turned to him, his angry expression slowly fading away as he remembered he had a customer who wanted food.

"I'll still give you five dollars." The American shrugged.

"Do not do that." I turned to the American, pleading with him not to give in to the awful man. "He is overcharging you. And he is rude."

The vendor hissed—*hissed*—at me.

The American held a finger up to the vendor.

"But I want the amount you would normally give a customer for that price." He explained sternly as he pulled out a United States bill and held it towards the vendor.

Watching the American, I was suddenly struck by the beauty of him. Not just that he looked like a fashion model, but that he was obviously older than I had thought when I first saw him. Slight lines formed at the corners of his mouth, I suspected from smiling and laughing for more years than I had known. The corners of his eyes had a few small lines, and his eyes had obviously seen more years than mine, though I felt his had been happier. He was distinguished and handsome, and obviously unaffected by the scene that had played out before him. My stomach fluttered again, though it was not about food for once that day.

The vendor was appraising both the American and myself, wondering if he should give in and admit that he had tried to gouge the man with the handsome face and amiable nature. Staring straight ahead, allowing me to examine his features, the American continued to hold the money out to the vendor, his expression unchanging. After several moments, the vendor made a noise, not unlike something *Ebenezer Scrooge* would utter when greeted with a cheerful *Merry Christmas*, the vendor reached over the counter and snatched the money from the American's grasp. Providing a mere smile in response to the rudeness, the American returned his wallet to his back pocket, his movements graceful and practiced. My eyes took notice of his long, elegant fingers, perfectly clean with manicured nails.

"Thank you." He said to the brusque vendor. "They smell delicious."

Finally, chastened by the politeness of the American, and knowing that further rudeness would only make him look more awful, he gave a nod and turned to complete the American's order. As though emboldened by being within the boundary of the American and his confidence, I continued to stare at his profile. The sharp angles of his nose and jaw made less severe by the plumpness of his cheeks and brightness of his eyes. Which was a weird thought to have about brown eyes, nearly as dark as my own, but there was an intelligence and warmth that radiated from them. Again, my stomach had another reason to flutter.

In an attempt to distract myself from thinking unwelcome thoughts about the American, I stepped away, knowing that at least the American would get a sufficient amount of food for the money he had given the awful man behind the counter. When I turned back to the tent that had been selling the coats, the red coat was being pulled down by the vendor there, and a woman was handing him money, Deflating, trying not to chastise myself for allowing a distraction to allow someone else to purchase the coat, I pulled my hands up into my sweater sleeves in an attempt to warm my fingers. An involuntary shiver ran up my spine as I tried to decide where to start looking for another tent that would be selling a similarly priced coat that would last through winter.

All around me, kids were running around, squealing joyfully as they played with the light-up toys purchased for them by their parents. Adults, probably the parents of said children, were strolling hand in hand together, or lifting giant bites of street food to their mouths. Steamy, food-scented air permeated the festival as the lights overhead twinkled whimsically, and laughter echoed from all directions. I flexed my fingers within the confines of my sweater sleeves and shifted my feet, trying to warm my toes, hoping that I could find an affordable coat before autumn spilled over into winter. I had gone without a coat in winter before, but I did not want to endure the snow and icy wind another year if it could be avoided. Maybe if I were able to afford good, warm meals with consistency, having a warm coat to protect my frame would not have felt so critical, but I knew that my life was operated on a "one problem at a time" basis.

Maybe I could have one plate of something inexpensive?

Then I could search for another tent with cheap coats for sale.

The dry toast I had had for breakfast and the meager portion of pasta I had managed for lunch had done nothing to warm me for the day.

"Here."

The sound of loud English, now very close, startled me, nearly making me fall over. As my head turned to find the source of the sound, though I instinctively knew it was the American, my eyes must have made me look crazed. An amused grin was affixed to his face, and he was holding something out to me. My eyes flicked downward to find a cardboard basket of the sugary, jam-filled donuts in his hand.

"I can't eat all of these." He said simply. "And you just had to intervene, so now I have more donuts than a human should eat in a year, so you have to help me eat them."

I found myself just staring at him.

"Okay." He gave a half shrug. "I probably could eat them all. But I shouldn't. So, I'm going to share them with you."

He jiggled the basket of donuts he held out to me.

Again, I found myself unable to speak, unsure of what I could possibly say to the American and his offer of free food. My stomach told me one thing while my reticence to trust anything another person, let alone a stranger, offered as a kindness tugged at my gut. Surely, this was a joke—a stranger, who was more attractive than a person had a right to be, offering to share anything with me.

"I didn't spit on them."

Smiling, I held up a hand.

41

"Non," I said, then corrected myself. "Thank you. That is kind."

"So," his brow furrowed, "is that a 'no' or a 'yes?'"

Shaking my head slightly, unable to keep a small smile from gracing my lips, I tried to mentally process the best way to express myself.

"I did not help you for free food." I finally managed.

"I didn't bring you free food for your help." He replied quickly. "I brought you free food because I have too much. So, I'm not being all that nice, really."

Again, I found myself frowning, considering this American and his offer of free donuts that my stomach was desperately trying to convince me to eat. The basket of donuts jiggled before me once again as I stared into his chocolatey eyes.

"I'll have to throw them away if you don't take them." He said. "And that will mean that I wasted money anyway, then it means that your help was pointless."

Over the American's shoulder, I saw the donut vendor glaring at me. For that reason alone, I slowly slid a hand out of my pocket, and tentatively accepted the basket of fried dough and sugar. Both my stomach and I wanted to do anything possible to rub salt in the vendor's wound.

"Thank you."

"Vous êtes les bienvenus." He replied awkwardly.

I merely smiled as I held the basket piled high with the treats.

"That probably wasn't great, was it?" He laughed.

"De rien." I said.

"What?"

"It is the same thing but easier to say."

"De rien." He parroted, and the attempt was admirable but imperfect.

"Very close," I said simply.

"Thank you." His head bowed slightly before he reached for one of the donuts in his basket. "You're not from Québec."

"No." I managed, though I suddenly could not bring myself to eat a donut in his presence, no matter how much my stomach screamed for it. "I am from France. I am Québécois now."

The man appraised me as he took a bite from the donut, which only made my stomach churn more violently.

"Immigrant," He said. "Your English is accented. Most of the people around here don't have an accent when they speak in English."

"This is true."

What else could I say? That I knew my French accent made my English atrocious at times? That, often, even Québécois had difficulty understanding my English? That even

43

my French was often mocked due to the fact that it was not precisely the same as my new countrymen and women? Admitting that I had an accent while most others did not was the only reasonable response.

The American popped the other half of his first donut into his mouth, chewing hungrily before reaching down to swipe his hand over the side of his pants like the fluttering of a bird's wings. He held his hand out with a smile formed around a mouthful of dough and sugar.

"I'm Peter." He said.

"I am Enzo," I said simply, almost forgetting to extend my hand.

Finally, I jerkily reached out and took his hand.

"It's nice to meet you, Enzo."

The man, Peter, smiled warmly as he swallowed his bite of food and shook my hand excitedly. The way that Americans do, which forced me to smile in return. Before it became imprudent, I slid my hand from Peter's and forced it into my pocket.

"Your hands are cold." He reached for another donut. "Are you going to eat yours?"

He gestured at the basket of donuts I held in my hand, close to my chest, as though afraid that I would lose them but also unsure of what to do with them. Peter was the type who stood closely to the person with whom he was speaking, but not so close as to invade their space. His tone was confident and measured while still sounding excited and friendly, no arrogance apparent. Our closeness allowed me to smell his cologne, which was warm, exotic, and musky, expensive and tasteful, and I could tell he knew how to apply such a thing without overdoing it. While he did speak with food in his mouth, he didn't try to chew and speak at the same time. I loved Americans. They were the antithesis to Catholic guilt— bold and unapologetic. Friendly and warm.

"Yes," I responded robotically, unsure of how to answer his first statement. I pulled my hand out of my pocket and reached for a donut, my stomach screaming out in victory. "Thank you once more."

Peter was already shoving the rest of his second donut into his mouth when I bit into my first donut. Sugary sweetness assaulted my tongue and lips, somehow both velvety and gritty at the same time, as warm liquid jam oozed from the donut. My eyes nearly rolled back into my head as I tried to remember the last time I had been able to have such a treat. Overwhelmed by the sensations flooding every fiber of my body, I had to force myself to not shove the entire donut in my mouth and swallow it whole. Then the next and the next and the next until the basket was empty and confectioner's sugar decorated my face in splotches, and jam stained my lips, leaving me looking like an Auguste clown in the middle of the festival.

45

"They're not bad," Peter suggested before leaning in conspiratorially. "But he's obviously way too proud of them, right?"

I couldn't help but laugh at that as I quickly stuffed the rest of the first donut into my mouth and reached for a second.

"There's this donut shop where I'm from." He continued as I took a ravenous bite of my second donut, almost forgetting Peter was there. "And you can get these jelly-filled donuts, kind of like these. Covered in powdered sugar. They're much bigger and not as round as these. One of 'em will cost you like, a buck, but they're nearly gourmet quality compared to this guy's attempt."

I gave an amused snort, sending up a cloud of sugar, which made Peter laugh. Though I felt I should apologize, I instead chose to stuff the second half of the donut into my mouth and reach for another.

"They're always the best first thing in the morning," Peter said, obviously aware that I was not going to add to the conversation until I had eaten the donuts. I knew I probably seemed rude, but I was just so hungry. "You have to go pretty early, like four-thirty or five o'clock. But they're warm and gooey. They'll melt in your mouth. Sometimes, if you get them really fresh, the jelly is so runny from having just been squirted into the donuts that it's messy as hell, but it's so worth it. I've ruined more shirts getting those donuts on my way to work."

My basket was nearly empty, such was the speed with which I inhaled my treats. Peter said nothing, but his eyes danced between the basket of donuts and my mouth, obviously aware that I was hungrier than I had initially admitted. I felt like a slob. Rude and boorish as I shoved donuts in my mouth, barely chewing before choking them down, simply wanting to fill my belly so that it would stop being angry with me. I was more than happy to simply listen to anything the friendly American had to say as I filled my gut with the food it so desperately sought. Peter could have told me that he was a serial killer and then laid out his modus operandi for selecting his victims, and I would have listened intently as sugar, dough, and jam slid down my throat.

"Do you want something to drink?" He asked when I shoved the last donut into my mouth, holding his basket with his remaining donuts out to me. "Because I would really like some coffee."

I eyed the basket in his hand as I licked my lips and rudely choked down the food in my mouth. Without hesitation, I took the food from him, sliding his tray into my empty one, and reached for my next donut. Peter watched as I scarfed down his remaining treats, in no rush to get a response to his proffered question. It seemed like only seconds before I was stuffing the last donut into my already full mouth, chewing and choking down bites of food like an animal. When the last bite of the donuts was sliding down my throat, my lips sticky and my mouth tingling from the sugary sensation, my throat raw from nearly swallowing the food whole, I looked up at him.

"Maybe a café?" He asked. "I could use a sandwich or something. A real dinner might be a good idea. Too much sugar and not enough real food and—"

He gave an exaggerated, jittery shake of his body.

"I am sorry." I slid my sweater sleeve over the back of my hand again, reaching up to wipe my mouth clear of sugar. "They…they were just so delicious."

He smiled.

"You probably need some real food, too." He suggested. "Something not made of fried dough and sugar, huh?"

I chuckled, suddenly nervous around this attractive American and his easy way of speaking with someone who was a stranger. Peter waited patiently for me to respond as though the night was not creeping in around us, the sun slowly going to sleep in the distance. It was as if he had nothing better to do than wait and see what I would have to say in response to his question. Though my parents had been patient people, most other people I had encountered up until that point in my life were not patient enough to wait for a basket of donuts at a festival, let alone give me time to make up my mind as to what I wanted to say. In English.

"I am actually trying to find a coat," I said, finally. "This is why I came to the festival."

Peter nodded slowly, as though suddenly understanding something.

"Oh."

"Yes." I gestured. "I was going to buy a coat from the vendor there, but someone just bought it."

"That's too bad."

I nodded in agreement.

"I am sure I can find another vendor, though." I began looking around, the empty baskets still in my hand. "I do not want to have winter come and not have a coat."

"Going to a store would be easier." He said.

I ignored his statement, knowing that I would have no luck finding a decent coat in an actual store and still have money left over for more food. Maybe a thrift shop wouldn't be out of the question, in fact, it was a good alternative to the festival if I couldn't find anything. Of course, with nighttime approaching, I would have to wait until the following day to visit a thrift shop if things at the festival did not turn out in my favor. One night without a coat would not be too unbearable, though I had often used my brother's coat for extra warmth at night since I was reticent to complain about the temperature of the apartment. My bills were already too high to allow myself the luxury of an apartment that was comfortably warm. I hoped that I would be able to sleep well, not having the coat at night like I had for the previous several months. It would feel odd sleeping once I finally went to bed again.

"Yes." I agreed though I offered no further explanation.

Peter was watching me once again.

"Thank you again," I said suddenly, realizing that I was wasting time. "For the donuts. They were very good."

"Made 'em myself." He winked.

For some reason, I found that very funny. Peter's eyes lit up as I laughed at his joke, as poor as it was. American humor, at its funniest, is nonsensical.

"You are a very good chef," I said, licking at the corners of my mouth.

"You got it all with your sleeve," Peter said. "Though I don't think much escaped your mouth."

Again, I was laughing, though this time, I felt warmth in my cheeks from embarrassment.

"I was very hungry," I said. "I am sorry."

"I'm glad you enjoyed them."

"I did," I said. "Thank you."

"You don't have to keep thanking me."

I had no response to that. No one I had ever met had said that "thank you" was not necessary when they showed you a kindness. Of course, my experience with Americans—while almost always pleasant, if not wonderful—was limited. Maybe it was uncommon in America for people to say "thank you" for something such as receiving food when you were obviously hungry. Peter tentatively reached out and took the empty baskets from me, but even that gesture seemed confident and controlled. I felt that Peter did not often find himself in situations where he felt completely out of his depth.

"I can throw these away."

"Thank you," I said, then cringed before a smile bloomed on my face. "That is nice of you."

Peter chuckled. "It was the least I could do."

As though neither of us had ever encountered another human being before, thus had no experience to guide us in how to proceed in finishing our interaction, we just watched each other. Peter continued to stare at me with his warm, curious gaze as if trying to figure out some riddle that I had posed. As the moments passed and the two of us simply stared at each other, I became more and more self-conscious of how I must have looked compared to my impromptu dining companion. Peter wore dark, stylish jeans, immaculately pressed and cleaned, stylish shoes made of what looked like actual leather (though I tried not to let my eyes wander over his body too obviously), the stylish, black wool peacoat, and the chunky gray scarf that had been wrapped around his neck in a Devil may care way. With his expertly styled and sleek hairdo, I felt insecure, and though that was not uncommon for me, the feeling was intensified when I realized how attracted I was to this man. My body began trying to make itself smaller like it had inside Mr. Paquette's makeshift classroom.

Peter gazed upon me, his lack of fear at being in that bubble of silence we had created emboldened me further.

"You can go with me to find a coat if you would like," I suggested nervously. "Then I can show you to a café for your dinner."

My companion smiled, the corners of his eyes showing their slightly crinkly skin once more, which brought a smile to my face. Peter made a grand gesture with the empty baskets, as though to imply that I should lead the way. A cloud of leftover confectioner's sugar rose into the air between us suddenly, making the two of us laugh and step back so as to not get covered in the powder, which would have been impossible to brush away. Especially from his black wool peacoat.

"Maybe I should throw these away first?" He suggested, coughing as he waved the cloud out of his face.

"That might be best." I laughed with him.

Before we left to find a coat, we found a trashcan, and in a silence pregnant with the curiosity we had for each other, we strolled away in search of a clothing vendor.

A Cross and Guilt to Bear

Kneeling, whether on the floor of the chapel or upon the kneeler attached to the pew in front of the row I had chosen, always left my joints sore and tight when my prayers were done. This wasn't because I spent an exceptionally long time praying, but because kneelers don't particularly do the job well for which they were designed. The old church that my family went to while we lived in France had attached a strip of cushion along the thin boards so as to make the experience a little less intolerable, though it didn't quite achieve its goal. In Montreal, the chapel I visited to say my daily prayers hadn't bothered with the comfort and slight luxury that a cushioned kneeler would provide. In fact, most of the pews did not have kneelers attached to the back of them at all. One was expected to kneel on the hard ground to say their prayers or stay seated in the equally hard pew to do the task. All one had to do was decide which part of their anatomy they wanted to punish.

At its core, being a Catholic is about suffering and being uncomfortable. Not to say that Catholicism is bad, nor do I mean to speak ill of my former religion, but you cannot be Catholic and expect to be comfortable often. Even in a family such as mine, where Catholicism and all of its tenets were more of a guideline than a strict rulebook, and we were much more liberal than the church found acceptable, there was discomfort. Guilt is the way most Catholics make themselves feel uncomfortable. It is our most popular drug. We feel guilty if we do not say enough prayers throughout the day. We feel guilty if we do not follow every teaching of The Bible—though no one seems to be quite sure which version we are supposed to be following—so we try and fail to follow them all. We feel guilty if we say something even slightly harsh about our parents. All day long, we weigh our souls down with guilt, and then we say our nightly prayers to ask for forgiveness for our guilt. As soon as we say our "Amen," we realize that we didn't ask the Lord to look over our mother and father and brother and sister, so the guilt begins again. If you do not feel guilt all day long, you are probably not a Catholic.

You also have to use the Lord's name in vain often, though you have to be sure that you are egregiously offended when you hear someone else do it.

Those are just the rules.

Often, I would find myself kneeling in church, either during one of the many services Catholics are expected to attend or just during my daily prayers, wondering if I felt guilty enough. Not because of something I necessarily did but for things that made me not worthy of God's love. Catholics are often told that we are imperfect beings, that we must constantly ask for God's forgiveness for one perceived slight or another. For some minor infraction we have committed without even knowing it or meaning to, which doesn't really matter.

My level of guilt increased exponentially when I was thirteen-years-old. That was when I first realized that I had no romantic interest in girls and that only boys aroused me. It was also the year that I discovered masturbation—on my own, of course, because, as I've said, my family was Catholic. So, feeling an attraction to boys made me feel guilty, but I also found that I had no interest in actually doing anything sexual with another boy, so I felt guilt about that, too. Why would I shame myself in the eyes of the Lord by being attracted to boys but only half-ass my offense? The Catholic version of God is so easy to offend, and I couldn't even adequately do that.

Being gay was a concept I was vaguely familiar with, so I knew what it meant when I felt attraction to boys. But the term "demisexual" hadn't even been coined then, so I had no idea that one could be gay with a hyphen. Of course, being Catholic, all you are taught is that there are gays, lesbians, and "*normal people.*"

Guilt, guilt, guilt.

My time spent praying stretched out longer and longer during the thirteenth year of my life, though I wasn't sure what

I was doing when I prayed for forgiveness for being gay. I was not actively gay, and no one had exactly provided a reason why being gay was a mortal sin, so my prayers were lengthy and vague. *God, please forgive me for being gay. I don't really know what being gay is all about, and I haven't even touched another boy in the way that I am supposed to touch girls. Please do not hate me, God. Please let my parents still love me.* That was my vague prayer that was repeated in my head ad infinitum from the moment my knees hit the kneeler until I rose once more and then in my head as I made my way home. While I ate dinner, while I had my nightly bath, while I told Noe a goodnight story, when I told Mom, Dad, and Grandmother "goodnight," and then as I drifted off to sleep.

I would wake up each morning with "I'm sorry, God" as my first thought.

All because I had done nothing.

Besides learning that I was gay and that masturbation was a guilt-laden, though wonderful activity one could carry out behind a locked bathroom door or in the dead of night when everyone else slept, two other major events happened in my thirteenth year of life. Our family of five became six when Noe and I became brothers to my sister. And then we emigrated from France.

Unlike Noe, Ila had been born in France, but like Noe, she had been unwanted by her parents and numerous families thereafter. This I learned at the same time I found out about Noe being unwanted and how some parents do not want their children if they are different. Though he could not express himself in a way that made it perfectly clear, I knew that Noe was excited that we were getting a sister when I talked to him about Ila's imminent arrival. Though I knew that Ila would be different, just as Noe had been, I was still thrilled with the knowledge that she would arrive.

Just like when I first met Noe, I didn't care that Ila was different—in almost the complete opposite way as Noe—I was just overjoyed at having a sister. Having both a brother and a sister was one of my prayers answered. Upon meeting her in our sitting room, another stern woman delivering her to us just as had been done with Noe, I saw that her facial features were quite different than those of everyone else in the family. When she spoke excitedly and happily, she spoke too loudly. She had a habit of laughing loudly at things that were really not all that funny, and she had trouble deciding when it was appropriate to speak and when to let others speak instead. Those things were what I loved best about her. When it was made clear to her that our parents were now also her parents, she was overjoyed. When she was informed that Noe and I were now her brothers, I thought she would fall over from excitement. She was older than Noe but seemed to need more guidance and care than either of us boys ever did.

Ila gave the best hugs I had gotten before or since, though I had to explain that she should never hug Noe. Mom and Dad dealt with the stern lady in another oversized suit while I took Ila to play and explained to her about not touching Noe or being too loud around him if she could help it. I told Ila that one day, he might allow her to hold his arm or be closer to him, but in the meantime, she should try to imagine a bubble around him and that getting too close would pop that bubble. Ila was such an excitable person that I was concerned that no matter how many times she was told that she would still disrupt Noe's happy environment. To my surprise, Ila was nearly as reverent as the neighbor's dog had been in regards to not touching Noe. Volume control, however, was another matter. But since Ila was respectful of Noe's personal space, he somehow adapted to her squeals and happy yelling. He would wince, but he tolerated the extra noise that came with Ila.

Church became a reason that I was glad to emigrate from France because Ila and church gave me another reason to hold Catholic guilt.

She is distracting for everyone else.

Some church members—not all, mind you, but some—are disturbed by her.

Maybe she can stay at home while the rest of the family comes to church, yes?

Mom and Dad would bring us all to church, just as they always had, but Ila found it difficult to sit through such long events without making noise or moving around a lot. She liked to try to talk to other people, especially to kids her age and other children, during church.

The looking down of noses, disgust on the faces of other members of our church, the whispers and stares. Sometimes outright animosity and displays of impatience by other Catholics at having to deal with a child who was different. Every Sunday, halfway through service, Mom would ask me in a hushed but unembarrassed tone to take Ila outside, down the street, to play so that everyone could continue through service without being disrupted. As I led Ila down the aisle, my larger hand holding her smaller hand, her cute little stubby fingers doing their best to clutch my hand, people would stare. Or roll their eyes. Shake their heads. Somehow managing to make disgusted faces at my sister, whom I thought was one of the most beautiful people I had ever met.

Ila and I would play tag and race a block away from church or see who could find the prettiest rock or spot the prettiest bird. Sometimes we would lie in the grass, and she would tell me about her new favorite animals—which was always giraffes—and I would tell her the story about her becoming part of her family. It was her favorite story besides the story of how Noe came to be my brother. As I told her these stories, I felt my most tremendous guilt as a Catholic. Not because I had done anything wrong.

But because I knew, without a doubt, that aside from my family, I hated everyone in that church. And I wouldn't feel guilty about that.

So, I felt guilty for not feeling guilty.

That is the cross that Catholics, and a brother with a sister who is different, just have to bear.

An Unaffordable Coat

Barely twenty minutes went by before Peter seemed to tire of my overly optimistic view that we would find another vendor who was selling a coat. Though the city is large—as cities tend to be—the festival itself could be explored in its entirety within that time. We had walked, mostly in friendly, though not entirely comfortable silence, through every street and alleyway where vendors had set up their wares. We had passed several food carts and tents, stalls lined with sweaters and t-shirts with big, bold words in French and sometimes English, booths filled with cheap plastic toys that made lots of noise and flashed lights, informational booths set up with literature about the city and province, and even palm and Tarot card readers. I was not the type of Catholic who felt that things like palm reading and Tarot cards were evil—my family had never been that silly, holding onto superstitious beliefs that crazed priests espoused as tools of Satan—but I felt paying money to know my fortune was a waste. After the years that had passed since we had moved to Canada, I was certain more of the same was to come. And if not, why pay good money to ruin a good surprise?

63

Peter, I found, was a person who loved to walk briskly, which was fortunate since my long legs tend to propel me forward faster than most. He had no trouble keeping up as I hurriedly strolled through the streets, shooting into alleyways on a moment's thought, or switched directions abruptly on a hunch. His breathing was controlled and healthy, the signs of a man who was not unfamiliar with exercise and efficiency of movement. My sweater sleeves became gloves as we walked, and I tucked my hands inside of them, desperate to make my fingers not feel like icicles. A few times, I saw Peter glance at my hands stuffed up in my sleeves, though he was kind enough not to ask questions or make comments. Nothing was said about why I had no gloves or an adequate coat for the weather, and he didn't ask why I looked as though I was dressed like a lead singer in a 90s American Grunge band. I was thankful for that because the answers to those questions involved giving away information that I not only wanted to keep to myself but would have humiliated me beyond the point of mending if I provided those answers.

Still, I forced myself to keep walking and searching, though I knew that everything I was doing was in vain. The red coat in the tent next to the donut vendor had been my one chance. Intervening on a stranger's behalf, simply so he would not lose a measly few dollars, had cost me my opportunity to be warmer throughout winter at a price I could actually afford.

A few measly dollars. Dollars were like gold coins to me, so how could I arbitrarily decide that this was not an important amount of money for my coat search party companion? With his exceptional coat and scarf, his expertly style hair and manicured hands, his expensive cologne, it would be easy to simply decide that he was a man with money to burn. However, maybe the five dollars he had spent getting donuts to share with me had been more money than he could have spared from his budget. He had mentioned wanting to find some "real food," but that did not mean that he had a lot of money. Dinner might include plans to pay with a credit card and then pay for it all later.

"What brings you to Québec?" Peter asked suddenly as I led us down a street that I immediately recognized as one we had walked down twice previously. "From France, I mean. Did you move here for college?"

"Non," I said. "We came here when I was in secondary school. Grade eight. I have finished college."

"You look so young."

"I am in my first year of university."

My heart skipped a beat as I thought of my studies and how time, money, school supplies, and responsibilities were making university nearly impossible to attend.

"Okay." He responded with a chuckle as he followed me. "It's obvious that I don't know anything about how school works here."

Finally, I stopped, right before we exited the street onto another. I turned to Peter, wanting to be cross with him for asking such questions when we had more pressing matters. My companion was looking up at me, a smile outlining the curiosity affixed to his face. Instead of being irritated, I slid my hands out of my sleeves so that I could shove them into my pockets and did my best to smile at Peter.

"I do not know anything about American schools, or I would draw parallels for you."

"What are you studying?" He offered as an alternative.

"Communications."

"How do you say that in French?"

"Communications. Or, *les communications*, I suppose."

"Huh." The corner of his mouth turned up. "You just have to give some things a French accent. I thought that was a myth."

I couldn't help but smile at that observation, though I found myself unsure of what else I could say to him. His red, wavy hair was distracting, and his upturned lip was enticing. I wanted his cologne to disappear like the smell of Noe's coat. That thought made my throat constrict.

"You're not going to find a coat at this festival." He said.

"Non," I relented, refusing to be angry that he said the horrible thought in my head out loud. "I will not. I will go to a store tomorrow."

Thrift store.

But I refused to be specific with Peter.

I would have to make sure that I did not eat anything else until I had found and purchased an affordable and durable coat the following day. Then I would feast if the budget allowed it. I would eat until I was sick and warm in my new coat. If I had close to half of my money left over, I would go to the dumpling restaurant underneath Mr. Paquette's ESL classroom, and I would eat until I ran out of money. Then I would sit in my seat and rub my belly and drink warm herbal tea and revel in the warmth of my new coat and the calories I had ingested. The thought made saliva pool at the back of my mouth once more.

"It's not that late." Peter lifted his arm to glance at the expensive watch around his wrist that I had not noticed before. The fact that he was wearing a watch amused me. Who wore a watch in the age of mobile phones? "I'm sure we can find a store that's open."

"I will go tomorrow." I managed to not sound too stern.

Peter shrugged.

"Then, I guess you have to show me where I can get a decent dinner." He said. "You promised to show me where a café was if I walked all over the festival with you."

I looked down, an embarrassed smile blooming on my face. Peter had been patient in following me all over the city center in search of something that did not exist. He hadn't even questioned me to find out if I possibly had a mental disorder or was under some kind of distress. He had trusted that I was a safe and friendly guy who just happened to appear as though he might also be homeless. Names of restaurants spilled through my head as I tried to decide where I would lead my companion for his dinner. It dawned on me that I had no idea what sort of food Peter might be interested in or whether or not he had a specific budget for his meal.

"What do you like to eat?"

"I'll eat just about anything." His hands went to his coat pockets. "But something that will stick to my ribs and make me sorry tomorrow will be best. I mean, I'm traveling, so I shouldn't eat responsibly, should I?"

I smiled at that. People who enjoyed food were my favorite people. Americans with open minds about food were even better. If they happened to be handsome Americans with beautiful red hair, it is even better.

"Is there," I began, unsure of how to politely ask an American about money, "do you want to spend a specific amount of money?"

Peter grinned wickedly. "I want to be sorry about that, too. But only if it's worth it."

I nodded, my smile growing wider.

Instead of directly answering, I began to move, indicating that Peter should follow me. He fell in beside me, his steps matching mine, keeping up with my pace, though I settled into a leisurely stroll since it was obvious I was no longer on a mission to find a coat. As we walked, I found my hands sliding up into my sleeves once more as I pulled my sweater tightly around myself. The city had not grown unusually cold for the time of year, but the lack of body fat I had then made any gust of cold wind feel like icy daggers against my flesh. Peter's frequent glances at me, huddling in my sweater, were hard to ignore, so I decided that conversation was the best way to distract him from wondering about my clothing predicament.

"You are traveling?" I asked.

"Yeah." He said, his eyes lighting up at my initiating conversation. "I'm obviously not from here."

I chuckled. "Why have you chosen Québec?"

"Well," he answered with an easiness I hoped to one day possess, "I'm actually here for work, so just saying that I'm 'traveling' might not be completely accurate."

"Oh?" I flexed my toes as we walked, hoping they would warm. "What is your job?"

Peter seemed amused by this question.

"Am I being rude?"

"No." He waved me off with a smile. "I'm a Financial Examiner. I dabble in forensic accounting from time to time. It's exciting to me, but a lot of people find it boring as hell. So, I don't talk about it much."

I raised my hands to the side of my head and pulled them outward, as though an explosion went off in my brain, as we walked along. Peter laughed as I slid my hands back into my pockets.

"I work for the U.S. government." He continued. "I check in on companies' financial records and make sure they aren't doing anything illegal…I'm like the money police. I also do some contract work."

"Money police?" I grinned widely. "That sounds much more exciting. You should tell people that is your job instead."

"Ya' know what?" He turned his head to grin at me. "I think I will. I mean, people will have questions, but at least I'll sound cooler."

"Very cool." I laughed.

We walked a few moments longer before Peter asked the inevitable question.

"Do you work as well?" He tried to sound nonchalant. "Or are you staying with your parents while you finish school?"

"It is just me," I said, simply.

"No parents?"

"Non."

"Are they back in France?"

I ignored the question. "I was working as custodian at a big...ah...*department*...store. But now I am cleaning for many different people."

How did I struggle with that word of all words?

"Why did you leave the department store?"

"I had difficulty getting to work on time," I said though I didn't really want to answer. He had been so open with information about his job that I hated to not give him some information about me, no matter how small. "I was taking care of my brother then."

"Oh," Peter responded. "Where's your brother now?"

I stopped, an exasperated sigh escaping my mouth against my will. Peter's movements stopped as well, and he turned to look at me, concern that he had offended me in some way etching his face as he looked up at me.

"It is just me now," I said, simply.

For a moment, we were staring at each other, and then his eyes grew sad.

"I understand."

I nodded.

"I'm sorry if I was rude."

"You are not rude." I shook my head and began walking again, though slower this time.

"Okay." He replied. "Even so, I'm sorry that it's just you now, Enzo."

"Thank you," I said. "I am, too."

We walked along the street, motorists and bicyclists passing sporadically, the sounds of the festival in the increasing distance, not speaking for several moments. It took me a moment to remember that we were walking, not to have a conversation and learn about each other, but for me to show him where a good restaurant was in which to have dinner. When Peter had first said that he wanted a hearty meal, something to "stick to his ribs" and make him "feel sorry" the following day, only one restaurant came to mind. When my family had first come to Québec from France, we still had money to spare, so after church each Sunday, we had a late lunch at a restaurant called *Le Canard Paresseux* – The Lazy Duck. It was a funny, whimsical name for such a nice restaurant, especially one that never seemed to have duck on the menu. However, they were known for exceptional, yet humble dishes, course after course being brought to the table until you were begging them to show you mercy. While not overly sophisticated, it was better than a café, and it was not as expensive as one of the many restaurants in the city that served tiny bites of food on larger plates than necessary while insisting that the diners should be grateful.

Travel is something that my family did not do in abundance. When we were in France, we usually stuck to the continent and quite often simply to neighboring areas of France when seeking new experiences. When we moved to Canada, we had never left the city, and by the time we thought of exploring our new homeland more, money restrictions—and the health issues of my grandmother made that impossible. When my father became ill, then my sister, and then my mother, it was impossible to even find dreams of travel a worthwhile pursuit. However, from what little travel we had accomplished, I had learned that many people will suggest restaurants or cafés to tourists that they think will feel familiar to them, thus desirable. I always felt that when one is traveling, they would want to try something different than what they may find in their homeland. Something that is warm and rustic, homestyle, yet with a flair that lets them know they are eating in a foreign country and trying new cuisine, even if the flavors are reminiscent of meals they've had before.

"Is this café open late?" Peter asked when we were nearly there.

"It is not that late." I frowned.

Without pulling out my mobile phone, which I did not want to do in front of the American as it was outdated and cheap, I knew it could not have been later than seven o'clock.

"Sorry." He shook his head with a smile. "The places I've traveled to recently roll up the sidewalks as soon as it gets dark."

"Roll up the sidewalks?"

"It's an expression meaning that the whole town shuts down when night comes." My companion chuckled. "I was recently in this tiny town in Texas, and you couldn't find anything but fast food unless it was Saturday or Sunday at dinnertime. I was between big cities when my rental car broke down, and I had to wait for a replacement."

My eyes grew wide with shock and horror.

"You may find some restaurants close on Sundays here," I said, "and sometimes Mondays, but on nights such as this—especially on the first night of the festival—they are open late. You will be able to take your time with your meal."

"Good."

Finally, I slowed until we were standing on the sidewalk, traffic passing slowly and regularly on the street before us. Across the street was The Lazy Duck, a fairly small building, tucked away between two much larger office buildings, with large front windows that allowed passerby to look inside and see how warm and inviting the dining area was, drawing them off the street. The building itself was rough stone that had been painted white many times over, with black shutters on either side of the windows, a large, rough-hewn wooden door painted black as well, and a large sign overhead, also black, that announced: *Le Canard Paresseux.*

"What does that say?" Peter's arm rose, his finger pointing at the sign.

"The Lazy Duck."

He chuckled.

"Am I going to be forced to eat duck?" He asked.

"Only if you ask for it." I laughed. "Though I have never seen it on the menu. Things may have changed since last I was here. They offer many things. If you are very hungry, they do courses with dessert or cheese to finish. The coffee is very good. I have never eaten anything that is not good here."

Peter's attention had been taken from the façade of The Lazy Duck, and he was looking over the tops of the vehicles that passed by, to the building on the corner of the next street.

"Hey, look." He said, pointing once more.

I turned my head, though I already knew what he had seen. A clothing store sat on the corner, also with large windows and sleek displays. It was a store that I never would have purchased clothing from, even when my family had money, because even at our best, we did not have enough money to entertain shopping there. Peter began to walk toward the crosswalk, obviously intent on forcing me to go into the clothing store that wouldn't even have a single item of clothing I could purchase for the money I had in my pocket. As I stood there, watching Peter walk with purpose towards the corner to find his way through traffic and across the street, I found myself with a choice to make. Peter now knew where a good restaurant was to have a delicious meal, so I had done what I had promised to do. I could easily walk away quickly, slip down an alleyway, and not have to explain myself. I wouldn't have to admit that I had no money for a new coat from an actual store. Or I could follow him to the store, say that I did not like anything that we saw, and leave without even so much as trying on a coat.

Watching Peter walk away, seeing the silhouette he cut in his nice jeans, shoes, coat and scarf—the way his hair ruffled in the breeze, I somehow felt that I would miss him if I walked away. Considering all things, I had not had someone to just have a conversation with in a long time who did not have preconceived notions about me. I hadn't spoken with someone so amiable and kind since before my brother had died. And I had never felt so attracted to another human being in my life, though I knew that was not the main reason that I wanted to spend more time with Peter. Being in his presence simply made me feel at ease, which was something I hadn't felt around another person for longer than I could remember. However, I didn't know what it would do to my soul if I had to admit aloud that I was one poor choice away from being homeless.

"Wait." I dashed after Peter; my mind obviously made up. "Maybe we can go after you have had your dinner?"

"The store will be closed by then." He waved me off with a smile as I came to stand beside him at the crosswalk. Peter was watching for a break in traffic so that he could dash across the street to the store. "Buying a coat won't take that long anyway."

Before I could say anything more, Peter had taken an opportunity presented by traffic and began to jauntily dash across the street, not a care in the world. My feet felt like lead as I forced myself to dash after him, dodging cars and hoping that something would make him give up on the clothing store. When we reached the sidewalk on the other side of the street, Peter continued until he was standing in front of the brightly lit display window to the right side of the entrance. I followed him, though even standing that close to such a chic looking store, with all of its straight lines and minimalism and lights, made me nervous. It was if I felt that in just being so close to the store, the gravity of it would pull the forty dollars out of

77

my pocket, yank it into its orbit, never to be seen or heard from again.

Peter made a whistling noise.

"Look at that." He said, his eyes on the mannequin in the window before us.

Though I didn't want to, I forced myself to follow his eyes to see what he had found. Inside of the brightly lit, nearly blinding display window was the mannequin, adorned in a sophisticated and expensive-looking navy overcoat. Unlike the red coat I had seen at the festival, I did not need to touch the sleeve of the coat to know that it was wool, nor did I need to inspect it to know that it was probably lined for extra warmth during the winter months. Just looking at the coat made me dream about owning such a garment, strolling along the streets of Montreal, a fat, stylish scarf wrapped in a carefree way around my neck, just like my companion. The forty dollars in my pocket might have paid for the buttons on the coat.

"It is very nice." I agreed.

"You would look very handsome in it, Enzo."

"Thank you." I felt my stomach flutter, and I refused to even so much as glance over at my handsome companion for fear that I would let on how much the compliment affected me. "It would look very handsome on you as well."

"Thank you." He chuckled warmly. "You should go try it on."

"There would be no point." I gazed longingly through the window.

"How much do you think it costs?"

"More than is my budget." I couldn't keep myself from answering, no matter how much it embarrassed me to admit that I couldn't even think of buying the jacket.

"Well, if it won't offend you," Peter said, "I'm going to buy it for myself."

Turning to him with wide eyes, I couldn't be sure if he was serious.

"You have not even asked the price."

Peter shrugged, an impish grin on his face.

Gross displays of wealth are normally a decent reason to become cross with a person, but Peter's display was not wrapped in an air of arrogance. Wanting the coat and resolving to simply buy it was a gleeful display of hedonism on his part. A way of saying: *let's do what we're not supposed to do*. I couldn't help but smile as Peter gave me a wink and turned towards the entrance with a wave of his hand for me to follow.

"I will wait here," I said sharply, though I was not upset.

Peter turned to me, a frown on his face. Looking down, I tried to indicate with my eyes how my clothes would look to the employees in the store.

"I am not dressed to go into such a place," I said. "They are more accustomed to dealing with people such as yourself."

For several moments, Peter stood there, barely a meter away, his face blank.

"You're not going to disappear if I go inside to buy the coat, are you?"

It was my turn to stare at Peter.

"I can wait if that is what you want," I replied.

Peter smiled. "Wait right here. Two minutes."

I nodded, and Peter slipped away, quickly sliding through the front door of the shop. Of course, I did think about disappearing, simply walking away from the store so that Peter could continue his evening unencumbered by some young man, barely out of his teens, dressed like a vagrant. Leaving just wasn't an option. The companionship, the easy conversation...*the kindness*...was addictive. If Peter had insisted, I would have walked into the store with him, even if the employees treated me the way that I looked.

As I waited, I found myself trying to catch my reflection in the window of the store. My hair, usually down past my ears, brown, with slight waves, was short that night. It had started to grow long after my last stay in the hospital a year prior, but when my mother became sicker, and then my brother, I kept it cut short. One less thing to worry about each day when I was getting my daily shower. Not knowing if my last stay in the hospital was really going to be my last kept me from letting my hair grow out. What is the point of enjoying one's hair if someone will shave it off haphazardly and unevenly once it has just grown out again?

Reaching up, I ran my fingers through my hair, feeling the ridges in the flesh of my scalp from where it had been cut into by doctors. Maybe one day, I would be strolling along the streets of Montreal, my own navy overcoat made of fresh virgin wool and fat scarf just the right shade of gray protecting me from the cold. In that dream, my hair was past my ears, wavy, and free in the wind. My nose would be frozen. My cheeks would be pink, though they would be plump from all of the food I would have eaten. I would have a paunch that pushed against the buttons of my new, fancy coat. I stopped myself when I began imagining Peter's arm laced through mine, walking with me and dressed in a similar fashion as we laughed over some nonsensical American saying.

Or maybe we would live in America? I began to wonder where Peter lived. What it was like in the city or town that he called home? Was there an autumn festival going on in the city square there? Would he have been buying donuts filled with jam and covered in powdered sugar from a street vendor that night if he had been at home instead of in Montreal? Or would he be at home, warming his feet by a fire, his beloved dog curled up beside him? Did he have a wife? Children? Did he have a sick mother or brother or sister whom he looked after when he was not traveling? Or…did he have a husband? I knew nothing of Peter and found that I wanted to know everything, though I knew it was pointless to learn too much about a person I would probably never see after he walked into *Le Canard Paresseux* to have dinner. While wearing his new, likely expensive navy overcoat.

"What do you think?" I jumped slightly at the sound of Peter's voice, nearly bumping my head against the front window of the store.

Peter cringed and laughed nervously as I turned to him. Embarrassed, but knowing that Peter had not meant to make me look foolish, I laughed with him. He was wearing the new coat. He looked very handsome in it.

"Très beau." I teased.

"Beau?" He cocked his head the side.

Before I could respond, Peter seemed to have a thought, and a smile bloomed on his face as his mental catalog of known French words answered his question.

"Thank you." He said, to which I responded with a nod.

Peter turned, giving me a chance to see how perfectly the stylish coat fit him. When he was facing me once again, I finally noticed that his peacoat was dangling from his fist.

"They did not give you a box or a bag?" I asked.

"I told them not to bother." He waved me off. "Come here."

"What?"

Peter didn't pretend he had patience for my question. Instead, he approached me and started to put the coat around me.

"What are you doing?" I asked, gently pushing away.

"You're worried about the way you're dressed." He said simply as I backed away, the coat falling from around my shoulders. "This will cover your sweater so that you won't feel self-conscious having dinner with me."

"Oh."

"I mean," Peter sounded unsure, "if you want to have dinner with me? I wouldn't mind having someone to talk to. Eating alone has gotten old."

I stood there, my hands cold, my toes cold, and certainly the rest of me more than willing to have a coat to wear, if only for a short while.

"I cannot eat dinner with a coat on," I said. "They would think that is odd."

Peter moved to put the coat around me again.

"You'll wear it into the restaurant and take it off at the table. Put it on the back of the chair." He said, slowly sliding the coat around my body. It was so warm. "Once we're seated, no one will notice your clothes anyway."

I allowed Peter to put the coat around me, and though it was a size or two larger than necessary, it felt perfectly wonderful. My arms acted of their own accord, tentatively slipping into the arms of the coat as Peter pulled it around me. As he pulled the coat around me, buttoning the front, as though I were a small child, I instantly began to feel warmer. Something inside of me wanted to pull Peter to me, hold him against my body. Being that close to him, smelling his cologne, watching the way he smiled down at his fingers while buttoning up the coat, made me want to be closer to him. Another part of me wanted to rip the coat off, shove it back into his hands, and then run away. I both wanted kindness and to reject kindness all at the same time.

It's an odd thing, the concept of accepting kindness. It is like a habit or an addiction. When you find yourself being treated equitably time and again, it becomes second nature to believe that all people are good. That no one in the whole wide world is bad. That you can always rely on people doing the right thing for others, simply because it is the right thing to do. When you have gone without kindness—and it does not have to be for a very long time, it just has to be consistent—you become suspicious of all kindness. You begin to think that anyone who does something even remotely kind wants something from you. Furthermore, you begin to think of accepting kindness as a weakness because you want to prove to the unkind world that you did not need sympathy from it anyway. You set out to prove that regardless of how the world treats you, things will be fine. So, when the world gives you a break, you tell it to go fuck itself. Just because you can.

I don't know if it was the cologne or the way Peter's eyes and lips looked when he smiled and buttoned up the coat—or maybe it was the ecstasy of feeling warm for the first time since I had lost Noe's coat—but I chose to accept kindness.

"Don't take this the wrong way, but I'm kind of upset with how much better than me you look in my coat." Peter quipped as his fingers let go of the coat, and he stepped back to examine me. "Très beau."

My cheeks felt flushed.

"It is a very nice coat."

"Thank you." He said. "I never knew it looked so nice, though."

Again, I found myself unsure of how to answer.

"So," Peter's voice sounded huskier than it had moments before, "do you want to have dinner with me?"

"I am hungry," I said. "Maybe we can find a more suitable place? So, we do not have to worry about my clothes at all?"

Peter just stared at me.

I made another uncharacteristic decision.

"I cannot afford to eat here." I shamefully explained. "It is not really expensive, but it is not within my budget."

My entire forty dollars would have fed me at The Lazy Duck, but I would have had nothing left with which to buy my own coat the following day or food to put in my refrigerator.

"I asked you to dinner." He replied. "That means I am going to pay."

"Non." I shook my head. "I could not do that."

"Sure, ya' can." He gave an incredulous laugh, and then his arm was suddenly around my shoulders, pulling me towards the crosswalk once more. "All you have to do is sit down, order some food, and eat it. You know how to use silverware, right?"

I couldn't help but laugh.

"Well, yes, but—"

"Don't make me carry the entire conversation." He said as he pulled me into the street when the traffic parted. "I'll talk about myself too much if you do."

"Okay."

There was really no way to protest Peter's insistence that I join him for dinner. But with his arm around my shoulders, I didn't want to anyway.

My Oldest Friend

For as long as I could remember, and even before that, I was forced to go to doctors' visits much more often than other kids and take medication daily. Sometimes I would take medication twice or three times a day, depending on the medication I was on and which doctor I was seeing. During the darkest times, I was taking so many pills in a day that I could barely eat due to the nausea I felt from the moment I woke up until I went to bed. Sometimes falling asleep and staying asleep was difficult due to how upset my stomach would be. None of the doctors seemed to be of the same mind and way of thinking when it came to my condition. My parents, my mother, a homemaker, and my father, a businessman, were not unintelligent or ignorant people, but they were not trained, medical professionals. We were at the mercy of the healthcare system wherever we lived and were of the mind that the doctors knew what they were doing. There was no reason to seek second opinions or get a referral to another physician or specialist unless it was suggested to us by the doctors I saw. So, my life and health were often governed by the whims of men in white coats or pajama-like scrubs who might be having a bad day and were rushing through their appointments.

Seizures were a side effect of the collection of extra, though benign, cells that formed a lump the size of a golf ball in my head, pushing against a vital part of my frontal lobe. From birth, it was apparent that my twitching and fits were not the normal behavior of a baby, and my parents soon found out about the tumor in my brain after several visits to the hospital. The medication I had taken for as long as I could remember was to keep me from having life-threatening seizures, and many visits to doctors only led to my parents being told that it was something we would have to endure. Though attempts were made over the years to try and surgically remove the tumor, to see if I could live without the medication and not have seizures, those attempts failed.

In the morning, before the sun had even begun to rise, we would check into a hospital. We would do paperwork, and I would be taken to a room. A needle would be placed in a vein in my arm, and my head would be shaved—usually, the side the tumor was on, but sometimes my entire head—and I would wait, doing my best to not cry or shake from fear. My mother and father would sit with me—sometimes my grandmother would join them—and they would do their best to keep my spirits up while I froze in the thin hospital gown. Then a doctor would come in, smiling widely, for it was not his head being sliced into, and tell us it was time. Then I would be wheeled away, my parents waving and doing their best to look strong as

I headed towards surgery. Strange men and women would stand over me in a room and prepare to make an attempt at extracting the tumor from my brain. The last thing I would remember would be a mask being put over my face and the world going blurry.

Sometime later, though, I never knew how much later until someone told me, I would wake up in my hospital room once more. My mother and father, seeing that I had woken, would rush to my bedside to hold my hand and gently kiss me on the side of my face. My vision would be blurry, and my head would hurt—not from my brain being poked at, as the brain has no pain receptors, but from my scalp being cut into and peeled back to expose my skull. I always knew that the doctors had abandoned the surgery due to the fact that I could tell that my parents had been crying. Once again, they had gotten bad news.

Every visit to the hospital, in an attempt to fix my problem, to make me "normal," only resulted in a shaved head, a new scar, and black eyes that did not go away for at least a week. Even after the bruises around my eyes went away, I would have to wait months for my hair to grow in enough to cover up my fresh and old scars. School could be torturous following surgery. Children love to point out scars and shaved heads and black eyes, and anything that illustrates how someone else is different in an effort to feel less different themselves. It didn't matter that once my hair grew in and the bruises went away, and the scars became camouflaged once more that the kids forgot about teasing me. Some scars, like the ones on my head, would always be there.

Over the years, I began to think of the tumor in my head as just another part of my body. Like a thumb or elbow—or maybe an unborn twin. We had been together since birth and would be together when my last day was done. I would have to take medication every day for the rest of my life in order to coexist with my oldest friend, but at least we could get along if forced. As I got old enough to make my own decisions about my own health, I decided that I would never have another surgery to try and remove the tumor. I was only taking one medication a day then anyway. Once my grandmother, father, sister, and mother were no longer with us, I knew that Noe needed me more than I needed to not take my medication. It wasn't that expensive anyway. And life was hard enough without trying to figure out his care while spending days or weeks in a hospital bed. Besides, after losing most of my family, I couldn't have another doctor look me in the eyes and tell me that my time had been wasted once again. That all I had to show for it was a shaved head, black eyes, and one more scar to join the rest.

My oldest friend and I would just live out our days together.

Though, after a while, I realized that my tumor was not my only oldest friend.

It was also the medication.

They were the two things I had left in the world that I knew would never leave me.

It was a comforting thought at times.

At least some things never change.

Le Canard Paresseux

Pushing the warm, stylish peacoat off to let it drape over the back of my chair was nearly impossible since I was afraid it would disappear like Noe's. Unlike Noe's coat, however, I knew that I would never be able to pay to replace it. If Peter's coat was grabbed by a stranger and they ran away with it, I would never forgive myself. In addition to the concerns I had about someone possibly stealing the coat— which was unlikely in a place like The Lazy Duck—I was still embarrassed by my clothing. Surely, even with someone like Peter sitting across from me, people would notice that, while my clothes were clean, they were not the best. My sweater was a little too big, the sleeves too long, my jeans had holes in them, though they could maybe pass as stylish. My canvas sneakers were obviously not meant to be worn out to dinner. With Peter sitting across from me, looking much more affluent than I, maybe people would think the worst. Maybe they would liken him to the man who had stepped out of the alcove of the closed store and offered me money after my prayers that one time?

Swallowing down my fear and reservations, I jerkily pushed Peter's coat off and let it gently fall onto the chair back. Luckily, The Lazy Duck was not so fancy as to have a coat check, so I had been able to wear my coat to the table. When the hostess had seen Peter and I arrive, she had glanced at me, completely unimpressed, though she had not been rude enough to smirk or sneer. Once her eyes moved to Peter, her expression changed to delight, such was the beauty and charisma of my companion. He had made her happy to see us with a mere smile while standing before her. I wanted that type of confidence and skill at making people want to be nice to me. Peter had requested a table for two in a corner, quietly telling the hostess that we were old friends with a lot of things to catch up on.

She had been more than willing to help him achieve that goal.

The Lazy Duck was softly lit and warm, with twenty tables and a few booths, most of which were not occupied that night. A four-sided fireplace was nestled in the center of the room, the flue reaching up to the ceiling. A bar was tucked away into the corner near the back of the dining area, close to the door that led to the kitchen, where beers, wines, and a few select drinks were prepared. All of the tables were of dark wood, roughly hewn but sanded and varnished to prevent splinters or unpleasant textures for diners. The chairs were well-cushioned and comfortable, considerate of diners who might choose to eat courses of meals instead of getting a quick bite to eat. The atmosphere was cozy and homey, though noise did not carry well, so it also felt intimate and snug.

My stomach did cartwheels when I smelled what wafted out of the kitchen and from the few occupied tables in the dining area. Once the hostess had seated us and handed us each a menu, she informed us that a waitress would be with us soon. Luckily, she had been much more polite than the donut vendor in the square. When she had heard Peter's English, she had replied in kind. I was grateful for that since I was too nervous to accurately and efficiently interpret for Peter. Having already endured my fellow students in Mr. Paquette's class previously in the evening, I did not want the humiliation of having the hostess do the same to me in front of Peter.

"How hungry are you?" Peter asked as his coat fell onto his chair back.

His new, beautiful coat that should have been hung from a hanger in the nearest fur vault.

"Everything smells wonderful."

"That's not an answer." He teased.

"I am hungry." I relented.

Peter perused the menu for a mere moment.

"I had an early lunch, and the donuts are the only thing I've had this evening." He explained nonchalantly. "I want to do the courses thing you were talking about. Let's go all out. Eat until we feel like we are going to explode."

"It may be expensive," I said, searching for something on the menu that was filling yet inexpensive. "They have many pasta dishes."

"Enzo."

I pried my eyes from my menu to glance over at Peter.

"I'm paying." He said firmly. "I can spend my money how I choose."

For a moment, I merely returned his gaze.

"I am sorry. This has been rude of me."

"You are not rude." He admonished me playfully. "You're being too polite. I want to eat until I feel like puking, and I want you to do the same. Okay?"

"Okay." I nodded, lowering my menu to the table.

"Are you old enough to drink here?" He asked. "We could get wine?"

"Yes. But no." I shook my head to clear my thoughts. "I have been able to drink for two years now. But I do not drink. I do not mind if you want to have wine."

Peter set his menu on the table as well and leaned into the table gently.

"How old are you?"

"I am twenty years old."

"Drinking age is eighteen here." He nodded to himself. "What twenty-year-old doesn't accept free booze?"

We laughed at this.

Answering Peter's question was something that I did not want to do, as it would give more personal information than I had been prepared to provide. Something about Peter made me forget all of the basic arbitrary rules I had made for myself in regard to interacting with strangers.

"I take medication," I said, simply. "Alcohol will…"

Peter watched me.

"The word…I cannot even remember the French word." I chuckled nervously as I searched my brain. "They do not get along?"

"Interacts?"

"Yes." I smiled. "Thank you. I am not supposed to drink."

"Then I won't drink either."

"You must," I said, gesturing emphatically, not wanting Peter to forgo something he enjoyed simply because I was unable to participate. "It is part of the experience."

"Are you sure?"

"Yes." I nodded. "Please. I am okay."

"Only if you're sure." He searched my face. "Okay. I will have a glass or two."

We both chuckled at this.

"But I guess I can't ask you for your wine recommendations." He teased.

I held my hands up and grinned goofily. The waitress arrived as Peter was laughing at my gesture, and he ordered a wine I knew nothing about, though I would soon find out it was a deep red. I asked for an herbal tea and water. Just thinking about sipping on a warm cup of tea after being out in the cold for the larger part of the day made me happy. Once again, Peter and I found ourselves unsure of how to continue our conversation, though I knew he had told me he expected me to help with that task. As we waited for our drinks, we stole glances at each other but mostly pretended to read our menus, as if we didn't already know what we were going to eat. When the waitress returned with Peter's wine and my tea and water, Peter asked me to order for us. I explained to the waitress that we wanted the whole experience of The Lazy Duck—which made her eyes light up since expensive meals usually lead to larger tips. She became even friendlier, letting us know that we should let her know immediately if we needed anything during our meal, then she left to put in our order for our first course.

"How often do you dine with strangers?" Peter asked as he brought his wine to his lips, taking a sip, his eyes closing in appreciation.

Before I answered, I brought my tea to my lips and barely even blew on it before taking a sip, which seemed to immediately warm my soul and make my stomach groan in appreciation. I knew that when the first bite of real food slid down my throat, I'd be in ecstasy.

"Not often." I finally replied with a chuckle.

"Is it rude to ask what you take medication for, Enzo?"

"Non. *No.*" I said. "It is so I do not have seizures."

"Oh."

"I do not have voices in my head." I chuckled, though I knew it was a bad joke.

Peter laughed with me.

"I am not dangerous."

"That's not very exciting." Peter teased, folding his arms on the table and leaning toward me in a too familiar way, though I liked it. "Isn't everyone a little dangerous?"

I considered this. "If necessary, I suppose."

"Necessary?"

"If you were defending your family from a burglar?" I replied.

He smiled. "Well, I meant, like, dangerous in a fun way."

"I do not know what you mean."

"Some people drink," He gestured at his glass that he had taken a mere sip from, "some people do drugs, or race cars, bungee jump. Those types of things. What dangerous thing do you do?"

"Have dinner with strange Americans."

He laughed.

"So, you avoid danger?"

"When I can." I nodded.

"Why is that?"

"Because life is…life is dangerous enough, yes?"

"Maybe." He relented. "But isn't it best when it is?"

I gave a small one-shoulder shrug. "This is possible. But sometimes the danger is not thrilling. Sometimes danger hurts."

I tapped my chest over my heart.

"I understand." He nodded slowly.

"So…no, I do not seek out danger."

"You must think I'm ridiculous."

"I think that you are charming," I admitted as my cheeks warmed. "I enjoy speaking with you, Peter."

It was true. Peter was being unashamedly flirtatious and probably not doing it well. Though, I would never have known the difference. I indeed found it charming, especially after all of his kindness.

Peter's laugh tapered off as he considered me.

"I'm thirty-nine years old." His face was blank.

I waited.

"You're twenty-years-old."

"That is correct."

"Should we be sitting here having dinner?" His eyebrow rose. "And should you be calling me charming?"

"It does not bother me."

"Do you understand my meaning?"

Of course, I understand. You feel that you are too old for me. And now I know that you probably do not have a wife and children.

"You feel that you are being a dirty old man." It was probably not the best way to explain that I understood his meaning.

Peter laughed sharply, chasing away my concern. His unwillingness to be offended made me find him even more charming.

"Yeah." He reached for his wine glass. "I could be your father."

"Impossible," I said, lifting my tea to take a sip. "My father is dead."

I hadn't realized what had come out of my mouth so flippantly until I had sipped my tea and set it down to find Peter staring at me, utterly aghast.

"I am sorry." I shook my head. "I did not mean to say that. It is just that…"

"Facts are facts?"

"Yes."

"Do you have any family?" Peter asked. "I know now that your brother and father are…gone. But do you have anyone else?"

Staring off at the wall for a moment, I considered the best way to answer his question. It dawned on me that Peter was comfortable with the truth.

"It is just me," I said, turning back to look at him. "My grandmother, mother, father, sister, and brother came here with me from Mantes. From France. They are all gone now."

"When did you immigrate to Canada?"

"I was turning fourteen." I had to think, as if it had been that long ago.

"Were they sick when you arrived?"

"Non."

"Holy shit."

"Yes."

"In six years? That has to be fucking tough."

"Yes."

Peter sat back in his chair, as though his whole body had been sapped of energy, as he stared at me with those still wide eyes. Seemingly unsure of what to say, I knew that I had to fulfill my end of the bargain, about keeping the conversation going. Not that I thought Peter would renege on paying for dinner, but I had made a promise to be his loquacious dinner partner. Talking about my dead family and my problems were not exactly the best dinner conversation, no matter how interesting a story it made.

"You are from the United States." I changed the subject.

"Yeah." He shook his head, as if clearing away thoughts, his eyes not looking quite like saucers anymore.

"Which of the states?" I asked, reaching for my tea. I wanted to drink more before it cooled too much. "Do you live in a city?"

"Uh, Minnesota." He said, bringing himself to sit upright in his chair once more, gathering his thoughts. "I'm in Minneapolis now. It's big like Montreal, though Montreal is bigger. Heard of it?"

I nodded, though I only had a vague knowledge of the city and state. My knowledge about the United States and the states themselves was not abundant then.

"I grew up in a small town." He said. "Which, I guess you did, too?"

"Not as large as Montreal, no." I agreed. "Is Minneapolis on an island as well?"

"I'm sorry?"

"Montreal is an island and a city," I said. "Montreal, the island, is surrounded by the Prairies River and the St. Lawrence River. And Montreal is a city on that island. Like your Manhattan in the United States, I think?"

Peter chuckled. "Huh. Ya' know, I never really thought about that. Though I guess I kind of knew that, too. But, no, Minneapolis isn't an island. It's just a bigger city. The Mississippi River runs through it, though. It's kind of close to Lake Superior and Lake Michigan, too."

"What is close?"

"A couple of hours?" He guessed. "You can go there for the day."

"Do you go there often?"

"No." Peter sighed. "I rarely travel just for fun anymore."

"Why is that?" I asked as the waitress appeared at our table with two plates.

She smiled and greeted us as Peter and I both sat back to give her room to serve us our first course. Warm roasted root vegetables and lentils with a turmeric and mustard dressing. My stomach wanted to do cartwheels. Once the waitress was sure that we were perfectly content, and had stepped away, I reached for my fork. Peter mimicked my actions but picked up our conversation where we had left off.

"I guess I'm just married to my work."

"Are you not married?" I asked. "Do you have a…spouse?"

He grinned as I shoveled a forkful of food into my mouth. Immediately, my taste buds began to sing, and my stomach begged for me to just swallow the food without chewing. It took effort, but my teeth moved into action. I promised myself to chew and eat like a normal person, to enjoy the meal as it might be my last really good one for a while. Besides, being in The Lazy Duck, and with Peter's kindness in paying, I wanted to act like a civilized human being.

"I don't have a wife back home. Or kids." He said. "I'm not that kind of guy."

"Okay." I shoved my fork back into my salad for my next bite. "I never let older men take me to dinner while wearing their coat."

"Understood." His grin grew. "I had a boyfriend until about a year ago. We lived together. Things didn't work out."

"Why? Why didn't things work out?"

"Married to my work. Remember?"

I nodded and chewed the warm, delicious salad, trying not to close my eyes in rapture.

"Do you have a boyfriend?" He asked, pushing his fork into his food once again. "This is really good."

"It is delicious." I agreed. "No. I have never had a boyfriend."

"Girlfriend?"

I smiled and gently shook my head. "I am not like that either."

"So," he grinned along with me, "neither of us is pulling one over on the other?"

"What?"

"You're a twenty-year-old gay man, and I'm a thirty-nine-year-old gay man having dinner together. No secrets or subterfuge." He noticed my confused expression. "Deceitfulness?"

"Oh. No." I agreed. "I am not trying to deceive you. But I do feel guilty for this."

"I don't want you to feel guilty." He said. "I'm enjoying your company."

"You are easy to talk to."

"Do you think that I'm a dirty old man?"

"No." I shrugged as I took another bite of food, my eyes on my plate.

"Would you be upset if I said I thought you were handsome?"

For the first time in my life, I set my fork down, ignoring food in front of me. I wasn't upset or embarrassed. I was overwhelmed. Though my English was decent, and I could easily carry on a conversation, I knew it would be hard to explain to Peter how I felt.

"I feel…" I laid my hands in my lap, my stomach in knots, though it was begging for more food, "I feel that I do not understand why you think that."

"Why?"

Looking down at my meager clothes, then back at Peter, I tried to make him understand.

"I did not help you with that awful man at the festival so that you would buy me dinner."

"I didn't buy you dinner for any reason other than you helped me simply because it was the right thing to do, Enzo." He stated gently. "You did a good deed simply because it was the right thing to do. I wanted to repay that kindness."

For a few moments, I allowed myself to stare at Peter to try and detect any hint of sarcasm or teasing of any kind, but nothing about him told me that he was being less than sincere. Finally, I picked up my fork and slid it into my salad again, my stomach feeling less tight.

"I wish more people were kind."

"People usually aren't kind to you?" He asked, skewering more salad for himself.

"People are usually not kind at all," I said, though my voice held no emotion. "People here are…they do not like the way I speak. Or my eyes. They think I am just poor immigrant who came here with my pockets empty and is congesting their city and living off of their public assistance. They think that I want things placed in my hand when I just want…I want…"

Peter stared at me, his forkful of salad halfway to his mouth.

"There is something I need to do after dinner," I said softly. "If you would like to come with me, that would be okay. If you need to go to your…hotel?"

"No." He smiled. "Where do you need to go?"

"I would like to go to church," I said, nearly embarrassed, but I decided that the emotion was useless at that moment. "I have not said my prayers today."

Peter stared at me for a very long time, his fork hovering over his salad.

"I can go to church with you."

"Okay." Another bite of my salad.

It was so delicious.

"What religion are you?"

"I am Catholic."

"Jeesh." Peter grinned wickedly. "I don't know now."

I couldn't help but laugh at that.

"I'll go to church with you, Enzo." He said again, his eyes radiating warmth. "But you have to do something for me after."

"What is it?" I asked cautiously.

"I never meet someone like you when I travel. A local who's so kind and handsome. You have to show me more of Montreal."

I smiled. "Okay."

"Great."

"I think you are handsome, too." I murmured as I skewered more salad.

Peter merely smiled as he dug into his salad, not embarrassing me by making a big deal out of my returning the sentiment.

No Hands to Hold

oving from France to Canada was an adventure, that's what my father told Noe, Ila, and me when my parents decided that my father would take a job in the Canadian province of Québec. For some reason, one that I still do not have a full explanation for, my parents decided that it was easier to move the entire family to Québec if we all became Canadian citizens. So, the arduous, lengthy, and costly process of moving to Canada and becoming citizens began. We found out that my father needed the proper credentials to work at his new job in Québec, we had to be permanent residents of Canada for a specific number of days within a five-year period, file Canadian taxes for three of those five years, and then we could apply for citizenship. The rest of us had to file paperwork to live in Canada with my father while he worked since we were not Canadian citizens. Later, after our move, we found out that Ila, Noe, and I did not have to meet the residency requirements to become Canadian citizens as long as our parents were in the process of applying for citizenship since we were minors, so the three of us became citizens within a few years of our move. My grandmother and parents did not live long enough after our move to ever become full citizens of our new homeland. Once all of my family was gone, I was alone and found out that I was a dual citizen of Canada and France, though I had no idea what to do with that information.

When I was left all alone in my new homeland, I had a barely furnished apartment, a few clothes, and the debt of my parents that I was, fortunately, not responsible to repay. Though, I was left with nothing to make a life of my own, either. I had no friends since it had been difficult for me to make friends in my new school. The fact that my French was sometimes odd to the students in my new school, and my English was weak compared to my fellow students made finding common ground frustrating. The fact that I had a brother with special needs, who did not look like he was my brother, and a sister with special needs, made me even more of an outcast. On more than one occasion, I was asked by other students what was "wrong with me." It was more than once that the school called my parents to complain about how I responded to those types of questions. To me, explaining to fellow students that there was nothing wrong with me—and there was nothing wrong with my brother or sister—even if I laced that explanation with a handful of expletives, was perfectly acceptable. The school thought otherwise.

My grandmother was the first in our family to leave us, though it was not as difficult to accept since she was older.

People die when they get older. It is a sad fact, but one that you cannot dispute. No one lives forever. Like my grandfather, she seemed to just get older and older in a space of time that seemed overnight. There were numerous trips to the doctor and a few visits to the hospital, and it was made clear to us that many things were wrong with her health overall, but none all that unusual for someone of her "advanced age." It was hard hearing that term: *advanced age.* My grandmother, while wrinkled and graying towards the end, never exuded anything but energy and warmth until she started to get sick. Then, seemingly overnight, she was no longer energetic and warm.

One night, she went to sleep, and the next morning, she didn't wake up.

It was odd, burying my grandmother in a foreign land that none of us were citizens of at that point. But there was really nothing else that we could do then. Cremation could have been an option so that we could return to France and sprinkle the ashes on my grandfather's grave or over some landmark that had meant something to her in life. But by that time, my father was ill. He was older than most men who had children my age, but he had always seemed younger, like my grandmother. Regardless of how he seemed, he was, in fact, ill, and the need to care for him and find a way to make money when he could not became our main priority. Thinking of taking my grandmother's ashes back to France just so that she could be near my grandfather seemed a waste of resources.

I'd like to think that my grandmother understood why she got buried in a foreign land, in a cemetery that none of her people were buried therein until later, but I am not so sure. Sometimes, when I think about what had to be done in the span of six years, just to ensure that someone in the family would be left, I am not sure of any of the decisions that were made. Those are not things you can change, however. I found myself dreaming that one day I would have so much money that I could have my family exhumed and cremated. Then I would personally take them all to France where they rightfully belonged. Or maybe I would keep them with me so that we would be a family again. Then I realize how morbid those thoughts are and push them out of my head.

On my best days, I am sad that I cannot speak to my family. Not just because I miss them all, but because I want them to know that I am okay. And maybe to let them know how much I miss them. Oftentimes, I find myself wondering how I have been allowed my years when my brother and sister, who deserved the opportunity so much more, were not allowed the same. Mothers and fathers and grandmothers are expected to leave you. But brothers and sisters are supposed to be with you, hand in hand, until the end. They are supposed to be there with you, holding your hand in old age, reminiscing about the good days past and the ones that are still to come.

But sometimes you reach out, and you find that there are no more hands to hold.

So, you have to hold your own.

The Things We Cannot Abide

Peter was quiet and respectful as he sat in the pew a meter away from me as I knelt on the stone floor, my hands clasped together, my head bowed, and prayed. At The Lazy Duck, we had finished our salad and then found our second course was a wild mushroom risotto, which delighted us both. We carried on with our easy conversation as we ate the second course, nearly going so far as to lick our bowls clean. Our third course was lamb chops atop white beans with a green tea sauce, and we hungrily dug into that dish as well. By the time the fourth course came, a plate of cheeses and breads with nuts and jams, our bellies were extended, and Peter was on his second glass of wine, looking rosy-cheeked and cheerful. Seeing him warm and well fed, amazed by all of the wonderful food made me happy. I knew that The Lazy Duck had been the right choice. Our dessert was dark chocolate gelato drizzled with raspberry coulis with an orange-scented Tuile nestled atop. By the time Peter paid the bill, which I had asked nothing about, we had eaten and drank more than we had a right to have eaten or drank.

We practically waddled out of the restaurant, feeling as though our coats would never button around us, though we managed the task admirably. As we waddle-walked down the street towards my favorite chapel, I wore Peter's old black peacoat, and he wore his new fancy navy overcoat. The coats were warm and protected us from the icy wind that had settled in after the sun went down, but the amount of food we had ingested probably would have kept us warm just fine. The walk to the chapel went by quickly, though we were both walking slower than usual due to the food in our bellies because Peter was telling me about growing up in the United States.

Though never interested in farming himself, he did, in fact, grow up on a farm in the western side of the state of Iowa, which seemed exotic and interesting to me at the time. Peter described to me the farmlands and rolling hills and plains, the bluffs and cliffs, and the many lakes. He told me about growing up carefree and running around barefoot during summers with his friends, then putting on heavy sweaters and coats and scarves during the often bitter, snowy winters. He spoke of building snowmen and making snow angels and snowball fights. He had no siblings, but he was fortunate enough to have neighbors nearby to play with during warm days in summer and snowy days during winter. Thanksgiving—held in November in the U.S. instead of in October like Canada—and Christmas were two of his favorite holidays, but Halloween was his absolute favorite.

Autumn held a special kind of magic and wonder for him, though he was nearly forty years old. Halloween was an oddity to me then, as it pertained to America anyway. Peter told me about carving pumpkins and hayrides, warm apple cider and haunted houses, costumes, and going door to door for candy bars, scary movies, and doing fun activities with friends and family. Most of it seemed like crazed rituals that even my wildest thoughts couldn't conjure up—but I wanted to experience all of it. From what I had seen in television shows and on the screen in cinemas, I knew that an American Halloween would be my favorite thing about the country.

Thanksgiving in America was an exercise in hedonism, it seemed. It was relayed to me through Peter that many people in America had the day off—which was always the fourth Thursday of every November—to spend with their families. Food was consumed in the form of meats and casseroles and any number of side dishes. Wine and beer were drunk with abandon, and American football and parades were watched on T.V. Families came together to show thanks but also to make complete asses of themselves. Peter's words, not mine. The following day, morbidly referred to as "Black Friday," was the start of the Christmas shopping season. Peter tried to explain the day to me, but it was so horrifying that my expression caused him to sputter with laughter whenever he opened his mouth to tell me anything about the day.

Eventually, he told me about Christmases and what they meant to him growing up with his mom and dad—both of whom were mercifully still alive—and the customs of his family. There was always a live Christmas tree, decorated with strings of lights with large bulbs and antique ornaments made of Mica glass that had been passed down by his grandmothers, the whole tree dripping with tinsel. Christmas Eve was always a big affair in his family, for that was when everyone got together for a big meal—and his family was big. They would eat until they were nearly sick and sing songs around a Player piano while the kids drank hot chocolate and ate sweets, and the parents drank wine and spiked cider. Then everyone would disperse, and Santa Claus would come in the middle of the night, so of course, Christmas morning continued the wonder and merriment.

While I didn't have much experience with Halloween or Thanksgiving—Halloween not being a big deal in France when I was a child—and Thanksgiving became a new holiday when we moved to Canada—I told him about my memories of Christmas. He was not surprised since we were headed to a church, that our Christmases revolved around our faith. There was Midnight Mass and Christmas Mass, of course, but we often spent most of Christmas Day at the church, usually at my mother's insistence. We would open presents very early in the morning, even though we had been to church so late at night, so we could get to church again later in the morning. By the time that all of the church-going was finished, we kids would rather go back to bed than to play with our gifts. But our home life and our Christmases were wonderful because our family had love. I told Peter about *Réveillon*, how it was like an American Thanksgiving, where people in France would eat course after course of food, stuffing their faces, and celebrate their togetherness.

I told Peter about how Noe had come into my life as my brother when I was barely ten-years-old, so I had experienced more Christmases as a child with him than with Ila. Explaining how Noe found it difficult to tolerate flashing lights and loud noises, so most of my toys could not have the batteries put into them, but we still had fun playing with them. When Ila came a few years later, Christmas became an even more joyous event because seeing the wonder on Ila's face reminded me of how joyful the holiday was for our family. Even though we had hard times, what with neighbors who didn't want Noe in their yard, and church members who were disgusted by Ila's Downs, we had each other. And I had never wanted more than that.

Well, that wasn't necessarily true.

I had wanted better lives for my brother and sister from the time they became part of our family until they were no longer with me.

Well, maybe not better lives, but a better world.

And I wanted my family back.

If I could wish for anything, it would have been those things.

"*And a new job that will pay my bills,*" I said while trying to cover my seriousness with a laugh.

When I told Peter this, he stopped in the middle of the sidewalk, disregarding the cold wind blowing sharply into us and turned to me. Turning to him, I found his arms pulling me in, and he hugged me right there in the middle of the street. At first, my instinct was to push him away, to reject his continued displays of kindness, to scream at him for being so wonderful when no one had been wonderful for so long. The desire to ask him who he thought he was, being so wonderful when I knew for a fact that people were not wonderful, was nearly overwhelming. Instead, I found my body melting into his, my head going to his shoulder, enjoying the warmth of him against me and the affection I hadn't had from another person in over a year. When I finally pulled back from him—he refused to be the first to let go—I had to wipe my nose and my eyes with the back of my hand, but he said nothing of it.

"Thank you." I had said quietly as we began walking again.

Peter reached out to grab my hand, to lace his fingers through mine, and I let him.

We walked along the sidewalk, holding hands as two men—a foreign concept for me at the time—and we didn't bother with caring if anyone saw it.

At the church, no one was in the chapel so late at night. Peter had asked in a hushed tone if it was okay to go inside so late in the evening, but I had explained that the chapel was open day and night for people to pray when it was convenient for them. Without another word, he followed me inside, down the middle aisle, and then into the row I always chose when I prayed. As I lowered myself into the pew, Peter sat down as well, though he gave me space as he looked around the chapel in wonder. As I usually did, I spent a few moments in quiet reflection, trying to gather my thoughts before doing my prayers. Once I felt quiet and peaceful, I slid from the pew to my knees to kneel, crossed myself, and rested my clasped hands on the pew back before us.

My prayers always began with telling God in my head—in French, as I still do to this day—that I hoped he was watching over my grandmother, my father, my mother, my sister, and my brother in Heaven. That he had known what he was doing when he took them. I hoped that they knew that I was okay and thought of them every day—that I loved them as much now that they were gone as I had when they had been with me. I asked that he watch over the people in the world who needed it most and that he show mercy to those who might need it. I asked that he continue to guide me and strengthen my faith, to help me to be kind and patient, to practice my faith in all things that I did. And then I asked God the one question that I had asked every day since Noe had left me.

Why?

I want to know why, God.

And I will ask every day in every prayer—in every language if I have to—I will learn every language to make sure you understand me if I have to—until I feel you have answered me.

I have always trusted in you, God.

But this I cannot trust.

I am a forgiving person, God.

But this I have not been able to abide.

Then I added a new message to my prayers.

Thank you for Peter, God.

Please look after him when he returns to America and every day thereafter.

Show him the kindness he shows others.

Love him and guide him so that he is safe and healthy.

I don't know if he even believes in you, but that doesn't matter to me, so please don't let it matter to you.

In the name of the Father and of the Son, and of the Holy Spirit.

Amen.

I crossed myself once more.

When I rose from my knees, sliding back into the pew, Peter was no longer sitting there waiting on me. He had disappeared.

And, for some reason, I felt panicked.

God Loves Dirty Feet

I was holding my grandmother's hand when she was dead. It wasn't the warm hand that I had held the night before, as I sat at her bedside, doing nightly prayers with her. She had been sick for months, though no one—the doctors that is—could ever really tell us what was wrong. She was nearly ninety-years-old, having had my father late in life, just as my mother and father had done with me. My grandmother was going to die, that was something that my parents and I knew, and I think Noe and Ila were mostly able to understand that would happen. When the moment would come, we weren't so sure, though we all assumed that she would get so sick that she would go into the hospital a final time, get sicker, and then never come home. When my mother went into my grandmother's room that morning after I did her nightly prayers with her, and found her dead, we realized that our expectations were not always what God had in store for us.

Memories of my grandmother are varied and many, reaching back as far as my earliest memories—the fuzzy ones that seem more like dreams than actual memories. In those fuzzy, hazy, dreamy thoughts, I remember running around on legs much shorter and plumper than mine are now. At birthday parties, holiday parties, family gatherings where food and love, not to mention God, were the main focus. I remember sitting next to her in church when we were in Paris visiting, smelling her powdery, flowery perfume, and leaning my head against her silky shoulder as the priest would give his sermon. I remember clutching her hand with both of mine excitedly as she would wink down at me as we stood for the Benediction of the Blessed Sacrament because I knew that it was almost time to leave church. Grandmother didn't care that I was more excited to get out of church than I should have been. She understood a child's need to run and play and tear the knees of their pants.

She knew that God understood that.

When we'd leave church, when I was very young, I remember that I'd immediately strip off my shoes and socks, glad to have my feet free from the tight, uncomfortable dress shoes. When my mom or dad would try to admonish me, she would intervene.

"*God loves dirty feet,*" she would always say as she took my shoes and socks from me, to keep them safe, as I ran off to play with the other kids in the park across the street. Sometimes, if my mother and father were not too upset with my childish displays, she would kick off her shoes and walk around the park with me, too old to play, but not too old to follow along.

Other than our love of leaving church so that we could experience the world that God created, which we worshipped in church, my grandmother and I shared our eyes. Though hers were more prominently almond-shaped than mine. Born in Cambodia, my grandmother met and married my grandfather, moving to France long before the Khmer Rouge takeover. She had avoided a lot of her country's strife during that period of time, but she also missed the connection to her culture and heritage, though she never spoke explicitly about it. She was happy in France, she adored my grandfather, as he was a good man, and she was positively enamored with my father when he came from their union. Because she felt so fortunate to have a husband she loved and was good to her, and a son who was the light of her life, she assimilated well to French culture. Anyone who spent time with her could feel the tucked away sadness at feeling removed from her heritage, though. I was one of the people who spent a lot of time with her.

Often, I would ask her to tell me what it was like in Cambodia, to tell me about food and clothes and customs, especially what Christmas was like in Cambodia because it was my favorite holiday when I was young. I was too young to realize that not everyone in the world was a Catholic, and I was so enamored with the holiday, that my grandmother would admirably sidestep the question—as she did with most questions about her heritage. I was always told that *one day* she would tell me about her life before France before she met and married my grandfather. That day never came. I often wonder if my grandmother had lived to one-hundred if she would have finally told me something...*anything*...that would help me understand more about my eyes. But that was a wish I knew to be pointless.

Catholicism was not exactly my grandmother's idea of a perfect religion, but she did her best to be devout because of her love for my grandfather. When I asked my grandmother about God and being Catholic, she would grow very quiet and take a long time to form an answer. At the time, I didn't understand why, but now I have realized it was because she never really saw herself as a Catholic, but she did not want to speak ill of something so entrenched in my family's history. Finally, after much staring off into the distance and consideration on her part, she would always say the same thing:

Be good to the universe, Enzo. And it will be good to you. What you give out is what you get back. That is where you will find God.

So, when my mother came out of my grandmother's room, a hand clasped over her mouth and tears rolling down her cheeks as she ran to find my father, I went to my grandmother's bedside and sat down beside her. My hand slid into her flaccid, cold hand, and I said a final prayer with her.

Because maybe if I told the universe about my love for my grandmother, it would show her love wherever she was. Even when my father's sobs suddenly rang out, sharp and sudden, echoing off of the walls of our house, I prayed for the universe to take care of my grandmother.

Hopefully, wherever she was, whoever was looking over her, they loved dirty feet, too.

The Kindness of Not Being So Polite

Peter's disappearance was not shocking to me, though I was panicked at the thought that seeing me pray had scared him off. Most people who are not religious can become uncomfortable around those who are devout. Assumptions can be made that we are planning to judge them or speak in tongues or…I don't know…slaughter a goat and ask for God to bless our house. My family was not that kind of Catholics. While we always did our best to honor God and family, to honor and respect others, to do service to mankind, to practice what we preached, we were not zealots. When I was approaching my teen years, and we weren't sure that we were moving to Canada yet, my mother and father sat me down. They told me that I would not be going to private Catholic school like a lot of my friends. They didn't trust the church to give me a proper education, and they feared that the biases would be thrust upon me. I was a little disappointed, thinking that they were treating me poorly, not letting me join my friends in school, but I have since realized that they were protecting me from a system they saw as profoundly flawed and troubling. They loved God, but not his bureaucracy.

As I sat in the church pew, making sure to breathe and not cry as I mourned the loss of Peter and his kindness, I realized that his kindness had come when I needed it most. If it was gone, I was going to have to be okay with that. I had received more kindness in one evening than I had received in many months. Maybe even years. So, I made sure to breathe deeply, filling my lungs with my gratitude for having met Peter. For my belly being so full that I wanted to lie down and take a nap before walking home to my own bed. A smile came to my face as I thought of how Peter had shared the donuts and then an extravagant meal. Like a lightning bolt, I suddenly realized that I was still wearing his coat. I rose from the pew, panicked for a new reason. I had to find him so that I could return his beautiful peacoat before he disappeared from my homeland.

Dashing through the chapel, which I never would have done, simply out of respect, I pushed through the doors and skidded out onto the street, the rubber soles of my canvas shoes squealing against the concrete.

"Where are you going?"

Startled, as though my spine would climb up and out of my shoulders, I spun around to find Peter behind me, next to the doorway of the church. He was leaning against the stone wall and sliding his mobile phone into his pocket as he held a half-smoked cigarette that glowed in the darkness of the church entry. My heart leapt in my chest—not from being startled, but from seeing that Peter had, in fact, not run away—and I had to take a breath before I could answer. If I responded with the first thing that came to my mind, which was *I was sad that you left*, I would have seemed weird. Taking a breath, thinking the moment through, I was able to respond in a way that did not make me seem so enamored with my new companion.

"You forgot your coat," I said.

Peter smiled and brought the cigarette to his lips.

"You used to work as a custodian, right?"

"Yes." I nodded slowly, still afraid to say too much too quickly.

"Would you have trouble getting to work now?" He asked, then his tone changed, as though afraid to say more. "Now that it's just you?"

For a moment, I just stared at Peter, wondering why he was asking such weird questions.

"I only have to worry about myself now," I said. "I am never late anymore."

I didn't tell Peter that sometimes I got to Mr. Paquette's ESL classes late because my tardiness was predicated on my fear of being humiliated by my fellow students.

Peter took a long drag on his cigarette, which made my mouth water. I had not had a cigarette in several months. I hadn't been able to afford them since before my mother had died, and even then, I limited myself to two a day. When I had first started smoking when I was seventeen-years-old, it was possible to have a cigarette anytime I wished. We had money then. But cigarettes had become a luxury I couldn't partake in anymore. I found myself staring at Peter's cigarette, transfixed on the glowing red tip, and his elegant fingers pinching the butt.

"Would you like one?" He asked, reaching into the breast pocket of his coat.

"Non," I said. "Thank you."

"Enzo?"

"Yes? My eyes were still on his cigarette.

"I would like to share my cigarettes with you." He said. "Do me the kindness of not being so polite, please."

Slowly, my eyes came to rest on Peter's. Nodding, I silently agreed. A moment later, Peter was lighting the cigarette that was held tightly in my mouth as I cupped my hands around the tip. When he pulled the lighter away, I took a deep draw of the cigarette, inhaling deeply, my eyes closing in ecstasy. Immediately, my head swam. I loved it.

Smoking was a habit that my mother had always hated, and on more than one occasion, she had hidden my cigarettes from me. On a weekly basis, I had gotten a lecture from her about the dangers of smoking and how God would not like that I was damaging my body with such things. Her lectures had never really interfered with my habit but made me more creative at hiding it from her. It was my one pleasure I allowed myself that was bad for me. I've since given up the habit, but at the time, most days, I thought about somehow getting a cigarette at least five times a day.

For several minutes, we stood near the entrance to the church and smoked. Smoking cigarettes so closely to the church made me uneasy and ashamed, as though God would be looking down upon me angrily for sullying the entryway to his abode. However, the alcove kept the wind, even though it was slight, from slicing into our flesh. Even with coats on our backs, the wind found cheeks and foreheads and noses and hands. It was unrelenting in its desire to chap skin and awaken the senses. So, instead of being ashamed, I smoked and stood with Peter, wondering what it was that I now had to say to this handsome American who had clothed and fed me.

"What does God say to you in there, Enzo?" Peter asked suddenly, relieving me of finding something to talk about.

"What do you mean?"

"When you talk to God—pray—does he ever reply?"

"I am not crazy."

"I don't think you're crazy." Peter smiled warmly. "I mean metaphorically. Do you ever feel something when you talk to God?"

I thought about this for a moment.

"Yes."

"What do you feel?"

Being asked such a big question made me realize how little I could explain my emotions and feelings about something infinite like God.

"I was raised Baptist," Peter said, obviously realizing that I had to think. "I've been to church hundreds, if not thousands, of times. I've never felt God there."

Bringing my cigarette to my lips for another glorious puff, I looked Peter in the eyes, wondering if he was mocking me or deriding my belief in God.

"Where do you feel God?" I asked, finally.

Peter smiled. "You really listen, don't you?"

"I like listening to you."

"I feel God when I have food in my belly." Peter began slowly. "When I wake up in the morning, and I have a new day to try again. When I feel the wind at my back and the sun on my cheeks. God seems to be with me when I take a long hike through the woods and hear his creatures and creations whisper. I feel God when I walk into a flea market and meet someone who does a kindness simply because it is the right thing to do. But, most of all, I feel God when I am able to buy a new coat and give my old one to someone who is looking for one."

It took a moment for me to realize what Peter had said, but then my eyes grew wide.

"I cannot take your coat." I shook my head violently. "It is too nice, and—"

"Does God teach you politeness, Enzo?" Peter asked. "When you kneel there and thank him for all he has given you? When you ask him to look over people?"

I just stared at Peter.

"Because being polite...*being nice*...is not the same as kindness," Peter said. "It's not the same as being good."

"It is not."

"Do me the kindness of not being so polite. Again." He said gently. "Please keep the coat. When we go our separate ways, I want that coat to go with you. It would mean the world to me."

"But it is so nice, Peter," I said, suddenly stricken with how lovely his name sounded rolling off of my tongue. "I know that it was not inexpensive."

"Who needs two coats?" He shrugged.

"I will have many coats one day." I nodded firmly, taking another draw of my cigarette. "My closet will be full of them. I will never be without a coat."

Peter's eyes locked on mine, and without so much as another word crossing either of our lips, I knew that we had an understanding. Outside of my chapel, where I did my morning and evening prayers, I actually felt that maybe God was listening.

"You never answered me." Peter cleared his throat. "Does God ever respond?"

"I do not talk to God." I sighed, a blue plume of smoke bursting from my mouth. "Not really."

"Who do you talk to?"

"I talk to the universe," I said, lifting my head, refusing to look weak or unsure of my answer. "Because all of this, all of these things," I gestured vaguely, "life is not between God and me. It is between the universe and me. I do not pray to a singularity; I pray to all things. I call it God, but it is bigger than that."

"Something bigger than God?" Peter asked, no hint of mocking in his tone.

"God is all things." I shrugged. "I have asked the universe to be good to my family. To my grandmother, my father, my sister, my mother, and my brother. I have asked it to help me find my way in this life. I ask it to look over and guide those who need it. I ask it to be kind to everyone. That is what I do when I am praying."

For the space of several breaths, Peter just stared at me. We continued smoking our cigarettes, flicking the ashes into the wind so that they might be carried away from the entrance of the church. After a few minutes, Peter knocked the end of his cigarette off and ground it out with the toe of his shoe. He was shoving the cigarette butt into the pocket of his jeans as I mimicked his actions, making sure that my cigarette was extinguished properly before shoving the butt into my pocket. Finally, Peter looked over at me once more.

"Have you gotten a response?"

"I do not want to talk about this anymore."

The response was a little sharper, a little bit more heated than I had intended, but the intention was correct either way. Speaking about God with Peter was not something that I wanted to do after we had experienced such a nice dinner. Both of us had eaten until we were barely able to waddle away from The Lazy Duck, smiling and laughing, speaking of beautiful memories, on our way to the chapel. I did not want my religion or God to ruin such a good time. They had already ruined enough things for me. Before Peter could make a comment about my pointed tone and my lack of tact, I affixed a smile to my face and slid my hands into the pockets of my new coat.

"Would you like to see the basilica?" I asked brightly, as though this would be the most exciting experience of Peter's life.

"The basilica?"

"Notre-Dame?"

"Like the one in Paris?" His head fell to the side, and he grinned oddly.

"Non. Not exactly." I laughed softly.

"What is the difference?"

"Geography?" I teased, and Peter laughed. "Basilique Notre-Dame de Montréal did not become a basilica until near the end of the last century. It was merely considered a church for a very long time. Notre-Dame in Paris is much older, and it is a cathedral—Notre-Dame de Paris."

"Oh." He frowned. "What does Basilique Notre-Dame mean, anyway?"

"Basilica of Our Lady," I said. "It is blessed in the name of the Virgin Mary. Just as Notre-Dame de Paris is Our Lady of Paris."

"Lot of Catholic stuff." Peter gave an exaggerated shiver. "I don't know if I can handle it."

I smiled at his comical behavior. "It is very pretty at night. Even if you are not Catholic."

"Will you hold my hand while we walk?"

Exhaling gently, I met his eyes.

"Yes."

Peter crooked his head to the side sharply with a smile.

"Then let's go."

The Things We Are Forced to Forgive

Montreal had been our new home for less than a year when I found myself searching my father out in our new house. Transitioning from French schools to Québec schools had not been nearly as seamless as my parents had led me to believe it would be. A shared language is not sufficient to consider two countries' cultures all that similar. Maybe if I had been merely white without *exotic*-looking eyes, students at my new school would have more readily accepted me. There wouldn't have been the whispers and snickers on the first day, or the elbows jabbed into my ribs, or the toes of shoes pushed into the back of my knee on the second day. I would have had friends to have break and meal periods with instead of finding a secluded area to avoid all human contact during those times. Other children—and even the teachers—enjoyed mocking the way I pronounced things in both French and English during classes.

Teachers would do this under the guise of frivolity and creating examples of how we could all improve our speech. Fellow students didn't depend on artifice to cover up their rudeness. They were proud of their bullying.

French, though a language shared by both France and Québec (and other countries and provinces), has subtle—and sometimes even significant—differences in usage between the two places. Just as the people of Britain and the people of the United States pronounce things differently, even simple words like "water," the people of Québec have molded our shared language to their own taste during years of separation from France. It is neither bad nor good that this has happened, it is just simply fact that a province that once belonged to a country, and separated by an ocean, will start to differentiate itself. Language is one of the first things that a province or territory will use in order to show its individuality.

Language was one of the first reasons that the other students in my class did not like me, or, at best, ignored me. Being Caucasian, like a lot of them, was not good enough since my eyes told the tale of my differentness. Often, I would be asked when I was going back to "where I came from." This would prove confusing at first since I had never known any other home besides France, regardless of what people saw in my facial features. I had never known the exotic landscapes or ecosystems of a country nearly ten-thousand kilometers from where I had been born and spent most of my life up until that time. Only two things connected me to my ethnic heritage— the part that was not strictly French and white—and that was my eyes—and my grandmother. One was something I had no say over, and the other chose not to do anything to provide me an education in my cultural and ethnic heritage. It was a frustrating thing, being "other," but not knowing exactly what that meant.

Never before our move to Montreal had I daydreamed of a land I had never known, but upon starting school in my new homeland, I found myself falling off into reverie multiple times throughout the school day. The library was a respite from the cruelty of school because there I could read about this almost mythical foreign land. Then I could daydream about mangrove forests and coral reefs, rolling plains and seagrass beds, lowland and upland mountains, monsoons and marshes and moist forests populated by exotic birds and reptiles. In my daydreams, my grandmother and I traveled Cambodia together, carefree and barefoot, mud sinking between our toes and local street food in our bellies as we held hands and breathed the thick, humid air. Somehow, I always skipped over all of the information about upheaval and strife in the country's history when I learned and dreamed about this land that somehow had a significant role in my life but also meant almost nothing to me.

Asking a person to personally connect to a cultural heritage that they have been separated from by distance, time, and silence is tantamount to torture. It leaves a person feeling half-fulfilled, half-realized, and perpetually confused about their place in the world. It is a cruelty of the highest order, expecting someone who has been denied an education about themselves to connect to that thing an education would have provided. It is like having a limb removed but never knowing that you had that limb at the beginning of your life. You just know that something is...*not right*.

My grandmother's funeral was to be held a week after she was found...not awake...that morning I held her hand and prayed. A few days after that morning, while preparations were still being made for my grandmother's services and interment, I found my father in his study. He was sat at his desk, a book opened on the desktop before him, his head in his hands as he stared down at the pages leafed open before him. Without asking, I knew that he was not actually reading the words. In fact, I was certain that he was not even seeing them. This was a moment of quiet reflection, a respite from the poorly timed gleeful screams of Ila, the nervous hand-wringing of Noe, and the sad sobs of my mother. Mostly, he was probably avoiding my stoicism. My non-reaction to what was going on around me was most likely the biggest thorn in my father's side.

"*Papa?*" I did not cross the threshold into his study.

My father didn't even jump. He merely sighed.

"*Entrez, Enzo.*"

Cautiously, I shuffled through the doorway of my father's study, as though I was afraid he would leap up from behind his desk and throttle me for having disturbed his quiet moment of reflection. Ignoring the armchair in front of his desk, I came up alongside it, choosing to stand and look down at my father. I could easily make my exit if my father became angry with me.

Before my grandmother had even died in her sleep, not long after we had arrived in Montreal as a family, my father had become withdrawn. He did not participate in family activities with any enthusiasm or commitment. He did not approach Noe or Ila for any interaction that was unnecessary, and, after a short while, he started to avoid me as well. I knew that his new job and salary were not what he had expected. My mother hadn't so much as said so, but she made allusions that this new job was not as well compensated, it was more stressful, and my father had become embittered by our move to this new country that none of us cared for in the least. Quickly, I ascertained that my father's new job was his version of my new school.

I wondered if he had any friends.

"*Papa*," I said, "*I was wondering…I was thinking that maybe we could take Mamie to Mantes? She would have preferred to be buried there. Next to Pépère. She would have liked that, Papa.*"

For the longest of moments, my father just stared up at me, his head still cradled in his hands. My hands began to sweat, and my spine seemed to be sliding down my back and trying to find a way out of my body through my behind. My father, so quiet and severe, made my blood turn to ice. I expected him to round the desk and cuff me on my ears, to shake me and call me a "stupid boy" or some other insult. Instead, he laid his hands on his desk, his fingers interlocking as he stared across that infinity of inches between us.

"I never wanted to be a father."

"Puh-papa?"

"My mother loved you more than anyone in this family." My father stated evenly, emotionlessly. *"Including me. I will never forgive you for that, Enzo."*

As though I had actually been punched, my stomach muscles constricted, physically causing me to hunch for the briefest of seconds as all of the air left my lungs.

"Your mother has cancer." My father said dismissively. *"And I am not well. We do not have the time or money to take your grandmother to Mantes. She will be buried here. Dans cet enfer."*

In this hell. That was what my father thought of Montreal. Our new homeland. Or maybe that was what he thought of our new home. I had neither the strength nor the desire to ask for clarification. My stomach was threatening to convulse again, but do more than make me hunch over.

"Yes…papa."

I turned to leave, my father's words ringing, not just in my ears, but through my entire body, sinking into my soul. Approaching my mother immediately with questions about what my father had said about her health was out of the question. Thinking of how my father hated me for his failure to nurture his relationship with his mother was all I could do. Now that his mother was dead, there was no rectifying an egregious oversight on his part. So, someone had to take the blame.

Though, I suppose that this bothered me little compared to his nonchalant statement about never wanting to be a father. Certainly, this stung for me, as his only biological child, but it hurt me more to realize that Noe and Ila had still not found two parents who wanted them. I could have marched into my father's study once more, demanded to know why he had bothered to have me if I was expected to be such a burden. Then I could have demanded to know why my mother and he had continued to add to the family by choice if it was not agreed upon by both parties. I could have demanded many things. I could have kicked his desk, shoved over his armchair, swung at him wildly, demanding to know why he mocked my pain by contributing more to what was becoming an insurmountable mountain. Instead, I silently closed his study door, letting him steep in the bitterness he had surrounded himself with like the many books on his shelves.

Sometimes, the only way to repay unnecessary cruelty is by letting a person fester in it. To let it dampen their spirits and poison what little joy they may possess. Cruel people are often most cruel to themselves…so they do not need others' help.

When my father died, not many months later, my mother and Ila were sick at home, both in their beds, trying to rest through their own respective pain. Noe and I were at my father's bedside in the hospital instead. Noe sat in the corner, staring, wringing his hands. My strong, warm hand clasped my father's weak, cold hand, and I stared into moist eyes as he stared back into my dry eyes. I didn't allow myself a single tear. But I forgave him, though he was unable to indicate that he had heard me. I didn't forgive him because he deserved it. I forgave him because it was something I believed I deserved. For, without knowing it, I had taken on some of my father's bitterness myself. I had allowed his anger and sorrow to shroud my memories of my grandmother in a veil of uncertainty. That was an unacceptable thing for me to allow to continue. So, I let go of it. Just as I let my father's limp hand slide out of mine after telling the universe that I hoped he would see my grandmother now.

In the span of a family's history, there are secrets and lies. Hidden jealousies and angers. Fears and frustrations and bitterness. And they remain hidden until a catalyst, usually loss, brings them to light. One family member, for fear of exposing themselves as human and vulnerable, will not say the things they need to say, to ask for the things they need to ask for…for whatever reason. A son may not ask his mother to be more affectionate towards him. A mother will not ask her son if she has been a good mother. A son won't tell his father that one sentence decimated his soul, which could only be rebuilt over years of practicing forgiveness. The reasons for these things do not matter. The fact that they are done does. My father allowed his soul to be destroyed because he had been unable to tell his mother that he felt he was not loved enough. My soul was provisionally destroyed by my father verbally striking out due to his grief. The details of why the timeline of a family includes these landmines are lost in the shrapnel and smoke left by fractured souls. Reasons and details will not fix anything. Forgiveness will.

I made sure—*demanded*—that my father would be buried next to his mother. It was my first big step toward forgiveness.

Hopefully, in the grace that comes with death, Heaven had two people who were beginning to repair any fractures that remained in their souls. And, maybe, a new pair of feet learned to love being dirty.

Basilique Notre-Dame de Montreal

The basilica was lit up, Gothic Revival towers looming down from either side of the building onto Notre-Dame Street West as we stood at the corner of Saint Sulpice Street. Stained glass windows depicting religious moments in the history of Montreal were lit cheerfully. One of the first things Peter had mentioned as he stood before the basilica, finally getting over the grandeur of it all, was that the scenes in the windows did not appear to come from The Bible stories with which he was familiar. Explaining that the scenes were the religious history of the city, as opposed to those depicted in The Bible, he accepted this at face value. Varying shades of blues, reds, purples, silvers, and golds sparkled out at us as we stood there, both of us with differing thoughts about what the basilica meant to us. For Peter, it was a historical and architectural wonder. For me, it was the grace of God, though I felt the pull less and less the older that I became.

"Jesus." Peter sighed as he looked up at the towers on either side of the building, then realized what he had said. "Sorry. I didn't mean to—"

"All Catholics do it." I chuckled. "We just have to act like we are offended when others do it so that we are still good Catholics."

"Well?"

"How dare you?" I gasped.

Peter laughed.

Our hands were still clasped, our fingers laced together as we stood outside of the basilica, though I knew my religion would not approve.

"Your hands are cold," Peter said.

He moved so that he was standing in front of me and grabbed my other hand with his, then brought both of mine to his face. Peter cupped my hands between his and leaned forward, blowing hot air into that bubble of flesh he created. I stared down at Peter, unsure of what to say as the warmth of his breath took the ache from my fingers. His eyes were on our hands as he began working on making me more comfortable, but soon, his eyes were on mine as he blew against my hands and began rubbing them with his own. There was something in my gut, and maybe in lower places, too, that twitched as our eyes connected. Peter stopped blowing, then brought my hands to his face, pressing his lips against them briefly, an ephemeral kiss before letting go of them.

"You," I stated hoarsely, then cleared my throat, "you are very handsome."

"Not as handsome as you."

I had to look down so that the flush of my cheeks was not on full display.

"Do you think somewhere nearby sells coffee?" Peter asked, letting me have my dignity. "I think you could use a warm drink."

"There is a place there." I pointed awkwardly in the direction of a shop further down the street, my eyes still down. "Would you like some coffee?"

"Coffee would be amazing right now," Peter said. "What better way to view the basilica than with a hot cup of coffee, right?"

"Yes."

"Here." Peter reached into his back pocket, extracting his wallet. "Let me give you—"

"I can buy two cups of coffee," I said gently. "You are going to wait here?"

Peter returned his wallet to his back pocket jerkily, his eyes avoiding mine as well.

"I need a moment." He said, a wry chuckle escaping his lips as he adjusted his stance. "Maybe you should go alone so that we aren't so close to each other for a few minutes?"

"Okay."

Without looking at Peter, I turned, my eyes still on the concrete beneath my feet, and began my journey across the

155

street. I had wanted to tell Peter that my body would undoubtedly miss his in the few minutes that I would be gone. The words were swallowed down to join the fluttering in my stomach as I crossed the street, which was usually much busier. Traffic wasn't nearly half as bad as it usually was due to the late hour. Soon we would be in that odd hour where people were starting to drift towards bed, yet it wasn't quite late enough to seem untoward to be walking about the city. Regardless of the hour, I did not care how unseemly it would be if someone found me walking hand in hand with a stranger along the city sidewalks. Peter could have asked me to walk until exhaustion overtook us, and we fell in heaps wherever we gave out. Or, if he had asked it of me, I would have gotten into a car and gone to the United States with him, such was his pull over me.

As I entered the shop down the street, rubbing my hands together to simulate the warmth of Peter's breath, I found myself ambivalent about Peter. Simultaneously, I wanted to tell Peter how enamored I had become with him in the space of a few hours, but also tell him that this was the strangest situation I had ever found myself in during my short lifetime. I did not have dinner or tour the city with strange men from foreign countries. Never once had I felt drawn to bring my body close to a stranger's, to want to feel any part of them touch any part of me.

Surely, Peter thought that I had been deceitful in the things I had been saying all night. He had given me a coat. He had paid for dinner and offered to pay for coffee. Peter surely must have thought that I was a male prostitute—a gigolo who was poor at his job but was still employed in the profession nonetheless. My dress was poor, I was young, I had no discernable gainful employment, and I had too readily accepted kindness from a handsome foreigner. Peter could not have been kind enough to accept the truths that I had told him at face value. As I asked for two coffees, black, and waited to pay, I realized that I would have to reiterate to Peter that I was not trying to have sex with him for money. Though, I found myself thinking about how sex with Peter would not be out of the question if he wished it. The thought did nothing to stop the fluttering in my lower parts.

What is wrong with you, Enzo?

In my twenty years of life up until that point, I had never considered actually having sex with anyone, let alone a stranger I had just met. Even boys in school that I found attractive did not have the pull required to make me consider doing such things with them. Why was I suddenly so enamored with someone I knew so little about? Yes, Peter was attractive. Yes, Peter was kind. He was charming and funny and generous. But he was a stranger. My body, especially the lower half, ached as I thought of Peter waiting outside of the basilica for me.

Thinking of his lips forming an "O" and blowing warm air across my hands made me flush. Up until that point in my life, I had never known what the term "sensual" had meant. Peter's mouth so close to my hands, warming them, then the flutter of his lips against my knuckles affected me in a way that nothing else ever had. When I had paid for the coffee, and I was carrying one in each hand out of the diner, my hands warmed by their heat, all I could think of was Peter's breath. The thought continued to do things to my body.

I have never been ashamed of my body. Though I have always been tall and thin—lanky and gangly—my body has always more than served its purpose. Walking across the street, trying—and failing—to hide my shame at what the thought of Peter was doing to my lower parts, was torturous. One can only walk so awkwardly for so long in an attempt to hide such a thing before the attempt itself draws attention to what it is trying to conceal. As I approached the curb on the other side of the street from the basilica, I looked up and found that Peter was lying on the sidewalk in front of Notre-Dame. With a horrified gasp, I clutched the coffees tightly in my hands and dashed across the street. Panic-stricken, I raced to Peter's side, looking down at him, wondering what had happened to make him fall in front of the basilica. It had been bitterly windy, but not icy. Had there been a puddle?

"You know," Peter said as I slid to a stop next to him and hunched over to look at him. "When you look at it from this view, I can almost believe in Heaven. It's like the towers are reaching towards God himself."

"What?" I gasped, still horrified that Peter had fallen. "Are you okay? Did you fall?"

"I laid down," Peter said, smiling up at me as he pulled his hands up to place them under his head. "I thought it might look even prettier from here."

"You did not fall?"

"No." Peter grinned wickedly. "I just thought I'd lay here and see if this angle is even prettier. It is."

"You—you laid down on the sidewalk to see the basilica differently?"

"Yes." Peter's grin grew. "Have you ever tried it? Looking at things from a different angle?"

Staring down at Peter, I remembered the coffees in my hands. Peter was grinning up at me, so I jiggled the cups at him sheepishly.

"I got the coffees."

"I see that." Peter nodded. "Set them down. Lay down and look at the basilica with me."

"What?"

"Lay down and see what I'm seeing. See it from a different angle. Please."

Looking around, I found that a few cars were still traveling Notre-Dame Street West, but the foot traffic was nearly nonexistent. The shop down the street had been empty of everyone except the employees, so no one was staring out of the windows, eating and wondering what was wrong with the guy sprawled out on the sidewalk in front of the basilica. Chewing at my lip, I glanced around sheepishly as Peter grinned up at me, enjoying my ambivalence in trying out this activity with him. It wasn't that I didn't want to lie next to someone so handsome and stare up at the beauty of the basilica, but years of making myself small so as to draw less attention to myself made me fearful of the activity. Finally, with a deep sigh, I knelt down and set the coffees down on the sidewalk above Peter's head. He smiled as I positioned myself, lowering my body to lie beside him.

As I shimmied my body into place next to him, he pulled one hand out from under his head to grab mine. I smiled to myself as I gripped his hand back and placed my other hand under my head to cushion it. Then I looked up so that I could finally see whatever Peter saw when he looked up at the basilica from his place on the sidewalk.

He had been right. Looking up at the basilica while lying on the sidewalk was a totally different experience than standing before it. When I would stand on the sidewalk and stare at the basilica, it was just a stone building with beautiful windows and jutting towers. On the sidewalk, staring up into the infinity of space and stars—what few could be seen through the light pollution—I felt like the basilica was reaching up to Heaven. All I could see before me was the building and the universe beyond. The buildings nearby, the light poles, street signs, cars…everything faded away, and I was left with Heaven and the basilica. Peter squeezed my hand.

"It's beautiful." I exhaled.

"Told you." Peter sighed, his thumb rubbing along the back of my hand. "I knew it would be prettier from this angle."

"Do you think the people who built it thought of this?" I asked.

It was a dumb question, but one I would have loved to have answered for me.

"I hope so." He replied. "I'd hate to think that they went to all this trouble and didn't bother seeing it from its best angle. Can you imagine anything more tragic than building something so beautiful but never actually seeing its true beauty?"

"That would be awful."

Peter merely nodded.

"Now I am sad."

"Don't be sad, Enzo." Peter turned his head to smile at me, drawing my eyes from the universe and over to him. "If they didn't see it from this view when they had the chance, they're seeing it from one we'll have to wait a long time to see for ourselves. At least they have that."

"You are…why are you so wonderful?"

"I'm usually not like this."

"How are you usually?"

"Morose."

"*Morose?*"

"Gloomy."

"I do not believe you." I smiled.

"Do you want to sit up and drink coffee?" He asked.

Nodding, Peter reluctantly let my hand slide from his as he sat up and turned to me, pulling his legs into the lotus position. I mimicked his movements. Reaching out, I grabbed one of the coffees and handed it to him, which he quickly cupped with both hands. Then I grabbed my coffee and used it to warm my hands as well. The fresh, hot coffee inside was easily felt through the paper cup that held it, which my chilled hands very much appreciated.

"I'm not like this, you know." He said. "I'm usually very sullen and gloomy. I don't like people, and I do everything I can to avoid having discussions with strangers."

"I still do not believe you."

"I'm married to my work because I don't have any faith in other human beings left," Peter added, ignoring my statement. "I like to be alone. I don't like compromise or negotiations. I don't like to worry about whether or not other people are happy with the way I lead my day to day life. Having to worry about relationships where part of the responsibility for making them work falls on me is absolutely excruciating. People do not want to be happy because that is when they are most miserable. People need conflict to feel alive. I don't like that, Enzo. I don't like people who are searching out the next struggle, the thing that will make them feel alive. I just like being alive. I like being with my thoughts. Alone."

"Then, why are we here?"

Peter turned his head, looking at the basilica, his head leaning back in an attempt to see it from our previous positions on the sidewalk.

"I don't think you're looking for your next struggle."

"No," I said. "I am not."

"I think you're looking to get rid of a few."

Nothing I could have said would have made Peter's statement more perfectly clear or accurate, so I brought my coffee to my lips and sipped it. The hot, black liquid warmed my lips and tongue, slid down my throat, warming my soul. It was strong. I loved coffee.

"I don't try to pick up strange men...anywhere." Peter continued. "I don't sleep around or make getting laid my life's mission. I want you to know that. I need you to know that, actually."

"Why?"

"Because I like you."

"I like you, too." I agreed. "I do not do those things either. I never have…"

Peter stared at me for a moment, then nodded, not requiring that I say that thing out loud. Again, he was secure in allowing me my dignity.

"I find it hard to believe that other guys don't chase you down." He grinned, finally bringing his coffee to his lips.

"Why?"

"I was lying when I said you were handsome, Enzo."

A frown immediately came to my face.

"Handsome isn't a strong enough word. Gorgeous, maybe? You're, uh, sexy."

My frown disappeared and was replaced with rosy cheeks and a smile I tried to hide by dipping my chin to my chest.

"I don't know why I am acting this way with you." He sighed. "But it is what it is. You make me feel exuberant. And you're gorgeous."

"Thank you," I mumbled. "I think you are gorgeous, too."

"Thank you."

"Is this ridiculous?" I asked. "Two strangers saying such things to each other? It is like we have been caught up in some magic spell."

"I don't believe in magic."

"Why not?"

"Because it would keep me from admitting what I know to be unequivocally true." He said. "I struck up a conversation with you because I wanted to. I invited you to dinner because I love your company. I'm sitting on this cold concrete drinking coffee with you because there is nowhere else I'd rather be in the entire world right now. Because I knew that you were put in my path for a good reason. This isn't a magic spell. It's kismet."

"Kismet?"

"Fate."

Laughing was not what I had intended, but I found myself laughing at such a proclamation from Peter. My head was thrown back, my eyes shut tightly, as I brayed at such a ridiculous, though sweet, thought. Peter was far too level-headed to subscribe to something such as fate. It was also ridiculous for a stranger to tell another stranger that fate had brought them together. Peter didn't get angry at my laughter but instead smiled at my amusement.

"Do you really believe that?" I asked once I had my laughter under control.

"Ask your God." He nodded up at the basilica. "While we're here and you have the chance to do so."

"Do you think that God would agree with you? Or do you think he would also think that this is too charming even for you?"

"I think God would tell you that there's no harm in believing."

There was really no response to that statement that I felt would be a sound argument. God definitely would suggest a leap of faith.

"So, it is fate." I agreed. "We were destined to meet at the Autumn festival. Now what? What happens after Fate has had its way with us?"

"That's the thing about Fate, right?" Peter leaned in with a wicked grin. "It sets you up and then just fucks off to bother someone else. It never really sticks around to tell you what you're supposed to do next."

I laughed loudly at this.

"Fate intervenes, but never ever sees things through. Fate is kind of the biggest deadbeat in the entire universe." He added.

"I suppose we have to be glad if it ever shows up then?"

"Exactly." Peter's eyes lit up, nodding along. "How tragic would it be if we were to ignore Fate? It only pops up to get things going. It's not coming back. Who are we to tell Fate to try some other time when things are more convenient?"

"I think we should spend the night together," I stated suddenly, unaware that I was going to say *anything*, let alone *that*. "I mean…what I mean to say…is that we would be reckless if we did not use this night to spend as much time with each other as possible."

Peter's face split with a grin, his eyes still sparkling.

"This is my only night left in Montreal," Peter said. "I would hate to spit in Fate's eye and not use every moment I have getting to know you, Enzo."

"I would—I would like to know everything about you, too."

"Then," Peter held his coffee cup out for me to tap mine against, which I did, "I think we should christen this as our first date. Would that be okay with you?"

My cheeks were warm again as I pulled my coffee cup back.

"That would be okay," I said. "It would be wonderful."

"I've never been on a date with a guy so gorgeous. Or young." He teased, bringing his coffee to his lips.

"I have never been on a date."

"Never?"

"No."

Silence overtook us as we both sipped our coffee, warming ourselves as best we could with the rapidly cooling drink. Peter just stared at me, though it was not awkward or uncomfortable. He merely seemed to be studying my face, as though he wanted to memorize every line since he would likely never see it after that night. So, I stared back, taking in the planes and angles of his handsome face. His fashionable swoop of red hair, the freckles along the bridge of his nose, the way his jaw was chiseled and masculine without being severe. I hoped, as my eyes danced around his face, that he found my looks as pleasing as I found his, though I wasn't sure if Peter was gorgeous to anyone but myself. I had never subscribed to traditional conventions of beauty, only concerned with the things I personally found to be beautiful. I hoped that I was beautiful in the way that Peter found most pleasing, even if it was not traditional or conventional.

"Do you want to see where I live?" I asked suddenly, then realized how that sounded. "I mean to say, do you want to see where I live in this city?"

Peter couldn't help himself, a wicked grin, which he tried to hide by chewing at the corner of his lip, bloomed on his face. Smartly, he lifted his coffee cup to his lips, sipping at it in an effort to further disguise his expression. Waiting patiently, afraid to say anything else about my meager apartment, I let Peter get his facial expressions under control

168

as he warmed himself with the strong, black coffee. Finally, he pulled his cup from his luscious lips, and his eyes met mine.

"I would like to see where you live."

"My home is meager," I stated softly. "I only say this as a warning so that you are not appalled by my home. I would just like you to know everything about me."

"I love that you want that, Enzo. And I understand." Peter nodded. "I'm sure your apartment is lovely."

"It is clean." I shrugged one shoulder, chuckling nervously. "But it is not lovely."

Peter laughed at this.

"I would expect nothing less from a former custodian." He quipped, which made me chuckle. "Enzo, I won't make fun of your home. And I would love to see it."

"Okay."

"Let's go." Peter stood suddenly and gracefully.

He held his hand out to me, and I took it.

Reasons to Keep Moving

The front door to my apartment, on the second floor of an old tenement building, would stick quite often. At first, it was an egregious annoyance, one that would frustrate me to the point that I would badger the landlord to fix it on a daily basis. Over time, however, I learned that pushing against the door while giving the bottom right-hand corner a sharp kick with the toe of my shoe would free it from the jamb. Whether it was set haphazardly in the doorframe or it was just old, thick paint that caused the problem, I wasn't so sure. Regardless, it was easier to deal with a sticky door than a landlord who felt he didn't have to fix anything due to the meager amount he charged his renters each month. The fact that he rarely gave me any trouble when my rent was late—which was often—also changed my habit of badgering him about the door.

The journey from the Basilique Notre-Dame de Montreal had not been long, but it had been electrifying. We were too busy holding our coffees and drinking them, as well as talking and wildly gesturing with our hands, to bother with lacing our fingers together once more. There was so much to be said to each other, so many things to learn, now that we had decided to honor Fate by taking advantage of the one night we had to spend with each other. Peter wanted me to tell him everything about myself, and I was equally eager to hear anything and everything he could tell me about his life. I wanted to know about his family, his traditions, his education, his likes and desires, his aversions and turn-offs, his favorite and worst memories—everything. And he wanted the same. Together, walking through the city as it slowly went to sleep around us, we shared the minutiae of our lives with each other.

Actually, the further I walked through the darkened streets of Montreal, a rapidly cooling coffee in my hand, I began to feel ambivalent again. Was I truly interested in learning every mundane detail of this gorgeous American's life, or was I so enamored with his kindness and charisma—not to mention his looks—that everything about him seemed thrilling? I hated to think that I had been swept up in the superficial nature of our new relationship if one could even call it a "relationship." We were technically on our first date. That in and of itself was strange. Who meets a stranger by chance at an Autumn festival and decides to turn the chance encounter into a first date? My mind went to the thought of dating apps and websites—one in particular stuck out in my mind—where people would meet up the same day they had learned each other's names through an electronic device, and pray that murder was not the outcome. There was something about

Peter that told me he would not harm me, though I knew he was dangerous. He had even warned me that all people are dangerous at dinner.

However, Peter was not a murderer or kidnapper. He didn't plan to rob me or ask me to do dangerous things that might result in harm. Peter was dangerous because he was too easy to like. Even if he had a horn growing out of the center of his face, I felt that I would have been enamored with him, begged to be in his presence for as long as possible. Maybe he had been telling the truth about being morose and sullen in his normal day to day life, but that was not the person he was in Montreal. I found him exciting and exuberant, thrilled to learn and experience. Quick with a laugh or joke. A lover of food and drink and walking instead of calling taxis. He appreciated simple things but reveled in the debauchery of spending money when one shouldn't necessarily do so. Most importantly, he hadn't been unkind to anyone the entire evening, even the donut vendor at the Autumn festival, though it would have been justifiable.

People who are treated poorly, whether that means they are spoken to rudely or not treated equitably, yet react with kindness are my favorite people. Kind people who know how to choose their battles wisely are vastly unappreciated. A considerable amount of willpower, and a strong sense of self are required to be that type of person. To not lash out in anger when a person has every right to do so requires great strength. Peter seemed to radiate that strength. He stood in the front room of my apartment, one of only three, besides the closet sized bathroom and walk-in closet-sized kitchen and stared at... *nothing*. Because there was not much at which to stare.

"You obviously clean thoroughly often."

I nodded.

"You don't have a couch."

"No."

"Where do you sit when you're at home?" He asked.

He wasn't judging me or mocking me. He wasn't trying to shame me. He was merely curious about me and my life.

"When I am home, I usually am sleeping," I said.

"It must be lonely." He looked over at me.

"Yes. Sometimes," I said but realized I could not lie while looking him in the eyes. "It is often very lonely. I do not like being here."

Peter allowed this statement to be what it was, neither diminishing the statement by doubting me nor amplifying it by pitying me. He simply let my truth be told without judgment either way—which is a luxury many people are not afforded. He walked further into the apartment, his eyes landing on the drying rack that had a few hand towels draped over it. His eyes moved to the kitchen doorway, which all of the kitchen could be observed through. He glanced towards the hallway. The paint on the walls was faded. The floorboards needed finishing. The ceiling had stains that no amount of scrubbing would chase away. Flashing neon lights from the street below illuminated my living room windows periodically, like demonic eyes blinking. Muffled laughter and raucous conversation drifted in from outside.

"It's cold in here."

"My landlord has not turned on the heat yet." I pointed at the radiator. "I think he will soon."

"Have you asked him about that?" Peter frowned.

I shrugged. "Rent is cheap, and sometimes I am late. He doesn't bother me about that."

A slow nod was Peter's reaction.

"What is it like where you live?" I asked as Peter's eyes traveled around the room once more, taking in every nook and cranny that contained the entirety of my life.

My life.

Faded wall paint and old floorboards, demonic neon eyes, and the laughter of strangers who were enjoying life more than I. It was humiliating. I wanted Peter to see all of it.

"I have a big house." Peter turned to me, his eyes landing on mine once more. "It's an older Craftsman home I restored a decade ago. Tall ceilings. Crown molding. Dark wood floors. Large windows that let in the sun and a kitchen way too fancy for anything I use it for. There's a big yard in front that is landscaped with flowers and hedges. The backyard is big and about the same, but with a nice patio and pergola for entertaining when the weather is warm. I had a barbecue built next to it that's nice to have during summer. A few large trees with huge leaves that are a bitch to rake during fall, so I usually get the lawn service to do it. Five bedrooms and three bathrooms. My bathroom off of my bedroom has a large tub big enough for two and a steam shower with a seat. I do a lot of thinking in there. It's a nice house."

I stared at him.

"Thank you," I said.

"What for?"

"For not lying to make me feel better."

"De rien." He gave me a soft smile, which I returned with my own.

Peter's eyes flicked to the space above my head, and I immediately knew what he had seen. Not that there was much in my apartment that I had to memorize the placement of since my belongings were few.

"Aren't you supposed to hang those outside?" He grinned, motioning with a jerk of his head to the bamboo windchimes over my head.

I chuckled.

"People on the street kept throwing rocks at them," I explained. "Ila loved them, and I was afraid that they would fall and be destroyed or that a window would get broken. Ila would have been devasted. So, I hung them in here. When she felt well, she could walk by and make them chime herself. Or, I could do it for her when she was unwell. She could hear them when she wanted to hear them most. She didn't have to wait for God or the wind to decide for her."

Peter stared at me, blankly.

I reached up, my eyes not leaving Peter's, for I did not need my sight to know exactly where they were, and brushed my fingertips lightly along the bamboo pipes. They bonked together, playing their distinctive sound.

"Can I…" Peter trailed off.

Waiting for Peter to finish his sentence was torture. I wanted to ask him what he wanted to ask me, beg him to finish his sentence. Was he going to ask to hold me? Kiss me? Make love to me?

Yes. Hold me.

Yes. Kiss me.

Maybe I will make love with you.

Well, probably.

I will definitely make love with you.

Anything you ask of me, I will do it.

Right now.

Just ask it.

Please. Please ask it.

You just have to say the words.

I have no real idea how to make love, but I will do it.

"I want to stare at you," Peter said. "Here. Where you do your living. I want to watch how you live when I'm not here."

This was more intimate and more embarrassing than anything I could have imagined. So, of course, I wanted to do it for Peter. But it was an impossible request.

"I don't live here." I slowly shook my head. "I...*merely exist here*. I am only living when I am walking. It is why I keep moving."

Peter's eyes were focused on the floor now.

"Even if I were to live here, I would be living with ghosts. Hollow, empty shells of memories of dreams unfulfilled and lives not allowed to flourish. Like flower buds sheared away before they were allowed to bloom. I would be living with the promises made by whims and empty gestures. It is why I only sleep here." I added. "If I do not leave here each day, I would not get out of bed. Unfulfilled dreams are very heavy. When I am here, I spend too much time in bed."

"Do you always sleep when you don't get out of bed?"

"No. Usually no, actually."

"Let me see that."

Fluttering in my gut, as though I might be sick, made me consider telling Peter that I could not do that for him. That

I *would* not do that for him. The fluttering and feeling of sickness had nothing to do with whether or not I could or would do anything Peter asked of me, though. It was my body warning me that I was going to expose my vulnerabilities to a stranger. I was going to crack myself wide open and trust that he would not pick at what he found within my shell. I was tired of my shell. I was tired of pretending that I did not have vulnerabilities. I was…just tired.

"Okay."

Without another word or any direction as to what he was supposed to do, I turned and began walking towards the hallway. I had taken a few steps before I heard Peter move to follow me. Together, in silence, we walked down the short hallway to my bedroom at the far end of the apartment, the one I had shared with Noe before…*before*. Without hesitating, because I knew it would make me change my mind, I nudged the door open, letting it creak loudly on its old hinges. That was something I usually worked hard to avoid, that long, eerie screech that reminded me how empty my life and apartment were, but Peter was with me. I let it sing its song. Everyone and everything has a story to be told. Sometimes you have to let it be told.

Within that small room, more like a prison cell than a bedroom, was my one bedside table, which held the few things I possessed that were frivolous. A few books, an alarm clock, a lamp, a half of small bag of potato chips I was portioning out daily as a treat, my cell phone charger that was frayed so horribly that I knew it wouldn't be long before it stopped working. There was the double mattress on a simple frame, no headboard. Luckily, the bed clothing had been washed recently, and I always made my bed each morning, so it was not unsightly. There was nothing else in the room except for my few articles of clothing in the closet.

"What books are those?" Peter pointed to the bedside table as we stood just inside the door of the room.

"Do you want to look?" I asked. "I do not mind if you look at my things."

"I want you to tell me."

Looking into his eyes for a sign of any type of amusement, and finding none, I nodded.

"*The Satanic Verses* by Salman Rushdie. *The Prophet* by Kahlil Gibran. And...*The Wizard of Oz* by L. Frank Baum."

"Are they in English, or...?"

"Yes. English." I answered. "They help me study the language more."

"Do you prefer French literature?"

"No," I responded. "I like American literature. Most of it is pointless."

"American literature is pointless?" Peter chuckled as he turned to me.

I thought about what I meant.

"I mean to say that often American novels do not tell a story where the point is obvious immediately. They do not bang you over the head. They seem unrefined and scattered, as though the writer is simply telling a story with no other intent but to tell a story, whether it seems well done or not. But when you take some time, it is obvious that the writer would be glad that you merely enjoyed a story, and would equally be happy if you took the time to analyze it. American literature does not put itself on a pedestal because it sees the value of reading simply to read. I appreciate that."

"That's an odd thing to say with *The Satanic Verses* on your nightstand."

"Salman Rushdie was born in Bombay, British India, and later moved to the United Kingdom, where he was living when he wrote the book."

"You got me there." Peter chuckled again.

For several long moments, I let Peter's eyes scan the room. I wasn't certain why it took him so long to take in the room, there being so little of it, but I allowed him his time. Outside, it was after midnight, and the noises from the street were louder than usual. Inside, it could have been any time of day, since, if it hadn't been for the noises on the street, we would have been lost to the world. Finally, Peter turned to me again.

"So, let me watch you exist, Enzo."

Ignoring his words, but not his request, I gently kicked my shoes off, using my heels and toes to do so in order to not have to bend over. My new coat…*my new coat*…was stripped off and hung on the edge of the door. Peter watched as I softly padded over to the bed and crawled onto the mattress, pulling myself up to my pillow. Turning over onto my back, as I usually slept at night, I did my best to get comfortable and ignore the fact that Peter was observing me. With a great sigh, I settled into my bed, trying to ignore the fact that this was an odd exercise. On a normal night, I would have crawled under the covers, maybe even started out on my side, facing away from the door, unafraid if someone broke into my apartment. Surely, they would not get past the front room before realizing nothing inside was worth their time. Normally, I would not be sleeping in all of my clothes with a strange American watching me from the doorway.

Lying there, staring up at the ceiling, I let my mind drift from the thoughts of Peter staring at me in my bedroom doorway. I forced my brain to do the things it normally did when I got into bed each evening. Silent prayers for my family filled my head. I thought of Noe and his blue coat that he had been so proud to wear. I thought of Ila and her rosy cheeks and boisterous laugh. I thought of my mother and her final words ringing in my head. I thought of my grandmother's dirty feet and the guilt my father probably felt in Heaven. I thought of the cruelty of the universe, taking my brother and sister from me. I thought of how I would pay my bills in the new month. I thought of budgeting my money so that I could eat just enough calories to get by each day. I wondered if I would need new shoes or a new shirt soon, or what would happen if my phone charger finally stopped working.

I don't know when the tears arrived, but like every night, they came. Fat, bulbous water droplets that grew in the corners of my eyes and rolled down over my temples, dripping off of my face and onto the pillow under my head. I'm a silent crier usually. There is no point in theatrics when one cries. The sting of tears and the feel of crinkly tear tracks on skin is enough to prove that one is sad. Tears and crying were a shame of mine, not because of some archaic belief that men should not cry, but because I wasn't sure who I was crying for anymore. Was I pitying myself? Was I crying for my lost family? Or, when I cried myself to sleep each night, was I simply too tired to force myself not to cry? It was my one time of day, unobserved, unbothered, unmoving, where my thoughts were allowed to overwhelm me, and I let them have their release, so I wouldn't be too tired to control them the next morning. When I had to face a world that cared not whether I merely existed or was living.

Just like I was unaware when my tears arrived, I didn't remember feeling Peter crawl onto the bed and curl up beside me, wrapping his body around mine. He hadn't removed his coat. He left it on so as to not give the wrong impression about why he was suddenly holding me. His head slipped under my chin, his face against my chest, as his arms went around me. My arms wrapped around him. I didn't force myself to stop crying. And the people outside continued to laugh and talk, as though a street full of buildings did not contain many lives and untold stories.

It's Not the Disease, It's the Treatment

L eukemia. Leucémie. It's not really a big English word. In French, it's no bigger. Four syllables in one language, three in another. Not that many letters. But it is a big diagnosis for a poor family with two members already missing, very little money left, and a sister with Down Syndrome who has already endured more than her share of problems. It is a hard word to have stuck in your brain when you are watching two men carry your family's sofa out of your apartment as your brother paces the floor, anxious and confused, as you hold one-hundred dollars in your hand. Maybe it would feed us for a week or two so that we had one less worry hanging over our heads in the tiny little apartment we had called home for a few months. After my father died, it was impossible to keep our new house in Montreal. A two-bedroom apartment—one room for my mother and Ila, one for Noe and me—with one bathroom to share, a kitchen the four of us could not comfortably be inside of at the same time, and a minuscule living room was what we could afford. Money would become an issue almost immediately after our move.

My first job as a teenager was as a custodian in a large office building where people wore suits and hurried about, doing obviously incredibly important things with papers held in hand and phones pressed to their ears as they marched through hallways. Luckily, my shifts were in the afternoons and evenings, when the office was at its quietest. I did not have to listen to the self-important proclamations from men who felt that having enough money to buy a suit made them important, even if their suits were always a size too large.

My mother was well enough then to make sure that Noe and Ila were taken care of and fed in the evenings when I was not there. She would make sure that they were taken care of and safe when I had to be away, but she was unable to understand how to help Noe with his hair. Because of this, even though I would get in late from work each night, I would get up early in the morning with Noe two hours before school so that we could maintain his hair. Only once or twice a week did we shampoo his hair together, depending on how dry it was, but every day required conditioning and putting oil on his scalp and hair. Noe had no problem styling his own hair afterward, but the products needed to maintain his hair's cleanliness and moisture were too overwhelming to his touch sensitivities. If Noe got the oil on his hands, he could not wash it off quickly enough to avoid at least a minor meltdown, which presented another challenge.

The challenges did not bother me, but the thought that he would have to face these impossible challenges simply because he had no help did. So, getting up extra early on very little sleep was something that I would do. It was better than waking him up when I got home to take care of his hair and depriving him of sleep. Out of the two of us, I was able to function on little sleep the best. Having the school calling and complaining to my sick mother about him being sleepy in classes or being "difficult" due to his sleepiness was something I wanted to avoid. My mother was not in a position to go to the school every time the inexperienced teachers didn't know what to do with a student such as Noe. And I needed to rest during the mornings and early afternoons so that I could be energetic and awake for work. The teachers never wanted to focus on how intelligent Noe was, how easily he grasped anything they told him—especially in his maths classes—but his perceived stubbornness they zeroed in on with wicked glee.

Two things about this bothered me. One, he wasn't stubborn. He was on the Autism Spectrum. The way he saw, processed, and coped with every day life's minutiae was different than the way kids without ASD did. He didn't have a bad attitude; he had a different disposition and mental process than his fellow students. Two, Noe was black. Anytime a teacher called him "stubborn" or "combative" or "rude," I couldn't help but wonder if this was not coded language for "black." If he had been a white student with ASD, would they have tried harder? Been a little more understanding of his special needs in a world that was not designed with his special needs in mind? Resoundingly, my mind always told me that my theories were correct. Especially since Noe was against hugs, except for when I came to pick him up from school when the teachers said he had to leave for the day. He hugged me on those days. And I glared angrily over his shoulder at the teachers as he squeezed me, burying his face under my chin. I never hugged him back, that was not acceptable to him—but he was happy to hold onto me in those instances.

Noe wasn't nonverbal. Sometimes he would talk a lot. But he only liked to talk when he felt in the mood to talk. He couldn't be forced to do so when he was having a difficult time, or on a day where he was particularly anxious—especially if he was having a day where breathing was laborious for him. *His moaning and groaning disrupt the class.* A black student with a medical problem and ASD was nothing but a disruption to the teachers at his school instead of being a student who needed more love, attention, patience, and empathy. Noe wasn't difficult. He was the easiest person to get along with that I knew, as long as you were willing to realize that your preconceived notions about how people should operate did not necessarily apply to him. The two of us could always meet halfway between our abilities and our needs. I could always find a way to calm him down and soothe him if he needed it.

Except on the day I sold our couch to the two men, and I had the word "leukemia" ringing in my head. People with Downs can be ten to twenty times more likely to develop Leukemia than most other people. That is something the doctors often fail to mention to families who have members with Downs. I don't know if it is because they feel it will cause the family undue worry, if they think that the family already knows this, or because they do not want to deal with the emotional and psychological fallout from providing such information. Of course, not telling a family means that they might shrug off a family member's night sweats or unusual chronic fatigue and weakness as being something else. For example, the symptoms might be attributed to someone suffering grief from the loss of their grandmother and father. Many families find out about the higher risk of leukemia once leukemia has encroached upon what was once a very happy life.

It was acute, the leukemia. And we were treated by the doctors as though this was something we should have expected, even been anticipating, so that we would have spotted the symptoms sooner. There were many things that I could say about my disappointment with Ila's health care. About her doctors and their lack of empathy and thoroughness in making sure we understood her particular challenges and health needs that were different from other teens in her age range who did not have Downs. In the end, it didn't really matter what we did or didn't understand about leukemia. Cancer didn't kill my sister. A massive infection—*a "complication"*—following a surgery to remove her spleen is what took her from us. Unlike the many times I had gone into surgeries and woken up to my disappointed parents, crying over my bed, Ila simply never woke up after surgery. We had to cry and hope that somehow, she would know how much we would miss her.

Going through the catalog of hugs shared with Noe in my memory, that is the only time I remember squeezing him back and not having him pull away.

Do You Want to Live or Exist?

Peter's crossed eyes looked enormous behind the reading glasses that were obviously made for someone with very poor eyesight. His tongue sticking out like a happy dog and his waggling head made him look even more ridiculous. Laughing at his ridiculous display—because it was funny—but also to keep from remembering how we had held each other on my bed an hour before, my laugh seemed to echo off of the walls of the cavernous pharmacy. Luckily, the two of us were the only customers present in the pharmacy so late at night, so there was no one to shoot me a worried or judgmental look. Peter cycled through a variety of increasingly ridiculous expressions for a few seconds, each one drawing laughter from me. Finally, he stopped smiling and stood up straight, his head tilting back so that his nose stuck haughtily in the air as he surveyed me from the other side of the display.

"Do these make me look sexy?" He asked in a grave tone, as though my response would decide my fate.

"Surprisingly, they do nothing to hide how handsome you are." I was blushing again, though I was smiling too widely at his previous displays to want to hide it from him.

"Just as I suspected." He waggled his head haughtily. "I must buy a pair for every day of the week."

"Stop." I chuckled.

Peter removed the reading glasses with a grin and a wink, then returned them to their place on the display.

"I guess the pharmacy is a happening place to be on a weeknight, huh?" He winked.

"Oh, yes." I gave an exaggerated nod. "The clubs are worried that the pharmacies will soon take away all of their business. As soon as they put in a bar and a dance floor—"

"You're ridiculous."

"I am ridiculous?" I laughed.

"Yeah. That's what I said."

"You are ridiculous."

"That's not an argument." Peter teased. "And it doesn't change the fact that you're ridiculous either way. So, if you were trying to defend yourself, you failed miserably."

"You are infuriating." The smile that came to my face, and my tone did not match the words that came out of my mouth. "Frustrating!"

"It's one of my many talents."

"Should I ask about your other talents?" I teased.

"Do you want the naughty ones or the family-friendly ones?"

"Hm." I looked up at the ceiling and pretended to consider this. "Tell me the family-friendly ones first, I suppose."

"Well," Peter leaned forward, folding his arms on top of the display to bring his face closer to mine. I did not move away, and had to keep myself from leaning in to put my face right next to his, "I'm a decent cook. I'm particularly proud of my mac and cheese from a box. I'm kind to animals and children that don't annoy me too much. I'm an exceptional typist. I rarely, if ever, trip over my own feet—no more than once a week. I've only burned my tongue on hot pizza a few dozen times in my life—so, super smart. I tip more than is required in restaurants and never stop in the middle of the sidewalk without moving to the side. I let people get off of the elevator before I try to get on. I read a book a week, so that proves how exciting I am. And…I'm a good snuggler."

My grin told him all he had to know.

"I like macaroni from the box. And reading is really cool." I said.

"We were meant to be together."

For some reason, my cheeks felt very hot.

That was the reason we were in the pharmacy. After I had finished crying on my bed in my apartment, with Peter snuggling up next to me, we silently got off of the bed and left. We didn't hold hands as we walked away from my apartment.

Peter's hands were in his pockets, and my hands were in my own. In silence, we walked along the empty streets of the city, in and out of pools of light created by streetlamps, letting what just happened sink into our brains. When we had been walking for what seemed like forever, Peter had spotted the all-night pharmacy and suggested we go inside to warm up and "maybe get a snack." I couldn't exactly say "no" to either activity. Being warm and eating were two of my favorite things.

"I mean..." Peter started to correct himself, then seemed to think better of it, "...no. That's what I meant. I think."

"You think?"

"That's what I think if it doesn't upset you." He smiled tightly. "If it bothers you, I was only teasing."

"It doesn't bother me," I answered quicker than I should have.

That made my blush deepen, and Peter's tight smile turn into a grin.

"What are your talents?" Peter asked gently, not removing his arms from the display. "Family-friendly or the naughty ones. Your choice."

"Well, I do not know what my naughty talents are." I shrugged impishly. "Yet. But I am a decent cook, too. I am proud of my instant noodles. I am kind to children and animals, too. Even if they annoy me. I love to read, though I probably read more than a book a week. So, I am much cooler than you are. I have discovered that cold pizza solves the problem of burning your tongue. I trip over my own feet at least twice a day, though I have only made myself bleed a few times. And…I like to write."

"You write?"

"When I have time."

"Anything I can read?"

"No," I answered too quickly again and had to correct myself. "I mean, I would be embarrassed. Nobody has ever read my writing except for teachers."

"What do your teachers think?"

"It depends on the teacher." I shrugged.

"What do you write about?"

"Life."

"Is most of what you write sad or happy?"

"It is both, I guess?"

"Life is both, right?"

"Right. And I have only ever written in French, so—"

"I might struggle to read it?"

"Yes."

"You speak English very well."

"My accent is horrible."

"It's charming."

"I wouldn't write in English well."

"I think you would."

"What do you know?"

"I know you would write well in English if you tried." He said. "I think you do anything you decide you're going to do."

"How do you think I became such a good Instant Noodle chef?"

"Enzo…" Peter trailed off again.

"Yes?" I wasn't going to wait this time.

"You make me happy I came to Montreal." He said. "Even if it was for work."

"I am happy you came to Montreal for work, too."

"Have you ever kissed anyone?" He asked suddenly, his cheeks looking flushed suddenly. "I know you haven't…but have you ever kissed anyone?"

"No." I breathed the word.

"Why?"

"I have never met anyone I have wanted to kiss before."

"What about now?" He asked gently. "Have you met someone now?"

"Yes." I breathed that word, too.

It was if I could not stop my tongue from telling the truth around Peter. Never before in my life had I spoken to someone so openly, unguardedly, and without caution. If I had been in possession of top government secrets and he had asked, I would have told him without hesitation. Maybe I had lied to Peter at The Lazy Duck. It was possible that I was a dangerous person at times.

Peter cleared his throat.

"This is unfair."

"What?" I asked, shaken by the sudden change in his tone.

"That we only have tonight." He replied sadly. "It actually physically hurts me to think that tonight will end."

He laid a hand against his chest.

"I do not like that thought, either."

Peter sighed, then suddenly he was out of sight, crouching next to the display on his side. When he popped back up, he held two packages of M&Ms in his hands, a wicked grin on his face.

"Snacks." He said simply.

"You should get Smarties," I said. "You are in Canada."

"Smarties?" He frowned comically. "I want chocolate."

"They are chocolate."

"What?" He produced comically wide eyes. "Smarties in the U.S. are these chalky disks that just taste like sugar that fruit was rubbed against."

I laughed.

"Smarties are just like M&Ms, except the orange ones have an orange flavor. Kind of. They are all chocolate, though."

"Why not both?" He shrugged. "I think I could eat a bag of M&Ms and a bag of Smarties."

"Box." I corrected him haughtily. "Smarties come in a box."

Peter waggled his head. "Faaaaaancy."

I chuckled as Peter searched the candy display, which was on his side of the aisle. After a few moments, he disappeared for a second again, then he rose up once more, two boxes in one hand and two bags in the other.

"Perfect."

"If these are awful, I will be very upset with you."

"Oh?" I folded my arms on top of the display and leaned towards him. "Will you have to punish me in some way?"

Peter's eyes grew wide in shock, then we were both laughing nervously, our cheeks a matching shade of rose red. Quite a few moments passed with our nervous, excited laughter echoing off of the walls of the pharmacy. Just as our laughter would taper off, we would look at each other, blush again, then start laughing some more. A few minutes passed before we could look at each other without laughing hysterically, but once we had ourselves under control, we made our way to the cashier to purchase the Smarties and M&Ms. When we exited the pharmacy, the city was still cold in the wee hours of the morning, but the wind had abated, making it much more tolerable.

We walked in silence down the street from the pharmacy, putting space between us and the bright lights of the signage and that which poured from the windows onto the sidewalk outside. The city is never all that dark, even in the wee hours of the morning, simply because of all of the businesses, streetlamps, and numerous other sources of light provided by modern-day technology. However, there is something equally tranquil and sinister about the city during such hours. Fewer people out and about means more silence, especially since the tall buildings create a buffer from the sounds from one street to another. Walks through the city can be enjoyed more at night since one is not expected to return smiles and greetings, adhere to social norms, or even pretend that they care about anyone but themselves. Without many people on the streets, though, danger seems to lurk at every corner, in every pool of shadow and dark alleyway. The experience of walking through the city at such an hour is exhilarating and frightening. It always made me feel alive.

"Where should we have our chocolate picnic?" Peter asked suddenly, interrupting my thoughts on the eerie quiet of the street.

"Anywhere." I smiled. "The city is ours, yes?"

"True." He gave me a glancing smile as he gestured across the street. "How about there?"

"*Parc La Fontaine?*"

"Sure," He said. "I mean, if that's what it's called."

I laughed.

"La Fontaine Park is closed," I explained. "People will not be allowed back inside until six o'clock, Peter. We will have to find another place to have our…picnic."

"Don't you want to be dangerous in a way that doesn't hurt?" He dared me with a wiggle of his eyebrows.

"But—"

"Who is going to keep us out of there?"

"There are fences."

Peter gave me an incredulous look.

"Okay." I relented. "A fence is not sufficient. But…what if we get caught?"

"I'm an American who wanted to see the park," Peter said, lacing an arm through mine and pulling me in the direction of the park. "You thought it would be a shame if I did not get to see it on my last night in Montreal. You were really just doing a service for city tourism. If all else fails, say I begged you."

I chuckled.

"No one would believe that."

"You'd be surprised what people will believe when they do not want to offend tourists and their money."

"Maybe."

"So?" Peter stopped in the middle of the empty street to stare at me. "Are we going to be dangerous? Do you want to live? Or do you want to exist?"

Peter knew the answer to that, so I was not required to answer verbally. His arm was laced through mine again, and he continued leading me toward the park, and I didn't resist.

Love Is Not Conditional

"*Well, that's it then.*" My mother's raspy, phlegmy voice came from behind me where she was perched on the bed.

Ignoring her statement, I gently lowered the lid onto the box and eased it down until it was secure. The box was no bigger than one a pair of large winter boots would have come in, but it held an entire life. It held years of a person's existence. Plain, brown, and unable to explain the memories and dreams held within, the last box of Ila's possessions sat before me as I knelt on the floor before it. All in all, three boxes of similar size, and a large bag had been sufficient to pack up what was left of Ila's personal possessions. Economics had left us all with very few things that we each called our own, and Ila was no exception, as was outlined by the packing I had done.

My head was throbbing, and I felt numb. My lips, mouth, and throat felt like a desert, and my eyes could not focus as my hands stayed atop the lid of the box. I wanted to swallow down my grief, but even that was too much to manage with how parched my throat felt. It was the crying. I had done so much of it that I felt as though there wasn't a drop of moisture left in my body. Whether or not my refusal to eat or drink anything over the previous two days was based on grief or self-flagellation, I wasn't sure. But my body felt withered and weak, and I did not know how I would manage to carry the boxes to a shop to be donated. I did not want to donate Ila's things, but I also did not know if I would be capable even if I had wanted to donate them.

As the strongest and healthiest and most capable person in a household, which has only half of its members left, one finds the world upon their shoulders. Choosing whether to allow oneself to be crushed under the weight or to continue to push against it is a difficult choice. My body told me to crumble, to let myself be pressed into the Earth until ever standing again seemed impossible, while my mind told me that my mother needed me more than ever. That filled me with rage that I did not have the energy to express.

I found myself replaying the history of my family in my head as I knelt there before the last of Ila's things. Other than my own health issues—which were more than manageable on the worst of days—my childhood had been perfectly ideal. Mother. Father. Son. Church and school and plenty to eat and clothes to keep us warm. A nice home with plenty of rooms to grow within when we had lived in France. Holidays with the little family we had and summer vacations that, while not luxurious, were always filled with fun and laughter. Somewhere in our timeline, the happiness had been stripped away, and our family began to shrink. Was it because my parents had been so old compared to other people with children my age? Had they waited so long to have a child that it was inevitable that I would not have my parents by my side later in life like most people my age? Had my parents overreached in adopting two other children with special needs, unaware of what was lurking in the years ahead? Had letting my grandmother move in with us driven a wedge between my father and me? Or had we, like a lot of families, been torn apart by the modern common problem of economic uncertainty, poor health and substandard health care, and the marginalization of immigrants (regardless of why they had migrated to begin with)?

All of the thoughts swirling through my throbbing skull left me wondering if anything I knew about my family was real. What did I actually know about my parents and siblings, and what had I just assumed based on my own youthful fantasies? Does anyone really know the people in their family—or do they decide that their parents are heroes, they will have their brothers and sisters with them into old age, and that no one in the family is harboring secret jealousies and angers? The question that banged around the loudest in my head was this: *what had decimated our family? Economic uncertainty and choices made without thought for the future—or our failures at never truly sharing who we were, not just as a family, but as individual people?*

What does bad health and death actually destroy if a family is united? It may cause sadness, of course. Grief is unavoidable, just like death. A healthy family, however, will always be able to look back on the memories and be glad that they had those times. But if that were true, that would mean that no one in my family knew each other at all. My family was a group of strangers, going through the motions. Waiting to see who would be the last angry and bitter person standing. Somewhere along the line, jealousy, disappointment, and anger had seeped in the cracks that death after death created.

"*Je suis gay*," I said, simply.

My mother was silent, but her breathing was not.

Even before my father had dropped his bombshell on me, my mother had surely been struggling. I had just not been aware. Children never notice their parents' declining health when it is not convenient for what is going on in their world. So, my mother's raspy breathing behind me reminded me of all of the times I had ignored signs that she was not well. The memories brought on a flurry of emotions that I was both not capable of and not strong enough to process. Guilt ran into rage ran into sadness ran into dread ran into acceptance. My family was dying. And I was gay.

"*Homosexuel.*" I shifted to look at her over my shoulder. "*Je suis homosexuel, Maman.*"

"I know." She said, a raspy inhale of breath followed by a cough that was quickly covered with her hand. *"I have been aware."*

"Okay." I turned away.

"Why do you tell me this?" She asked. *"Now?"*

"You know why."

"Because I am dying."

"Yes."

"Your father, grandmother, and I knew, Enzo."

"Okay."

"Are you asking for me to absolve you of your perceived sin?"

"I don't know what I am asking, Maman."

We sat in silence, the weight of our religion, past and current circumstances, the timing of my statement, and Ila's deafening, boxed up memories between us. In the archives of my mind, I pulled out files of my mother sitting in pews as priests proclaimed that the Devil resided within homosexuals. I examined the index of all of the times we had prayed that people with such twisted perversions in their minds found their way to the one true God through Christ. Though, they surely would never be forgiven. Not even in confession. Encyclopedias of how homosexuals would be punished in a God-less Hell flashed through my mind's eyes. I thought of how Downs could not be accepted by our church—our religion—how could my homosexuality be any different? And

Ila had been the purest soul I'd ever known. Quick to laugh, to offer a hug, to hold a hand, to tell someone they were pretty, to want to be friends. The first to look up at the stained-glass windows and whisper in awe: *"Magnifique."*

With a strength I didn't know I still possessed, I picked up Ila's box of things, hoisted it over my head in a rage, and threw it at the wall. The box split open, books and trinkets clattering to the ground, her favorite Christmas ornament exploding into a million tiny pieces. Just like our family. Just as quickly as the rage overtook me, I laid my hands back on my thighs and continued to kneel there amongst the wreckage that was now another life unfulfilled. If someone had approached me and thrown a fist into my gut, I wouldn't have reacted. I would have merely toppled over and prayed for God to put me in the Earth as well.

I could hear Noe making his distressed groaning noise in the living room, the one he always made when he was anxious and scared. Normally, I would have rushed to him and comforted him. But I couldn't. I was rooted.

If you were to examine my childhood, or at least the second half, the part where I had been blessed with a brother and a sister, two things would stand out. One, my brother was my best friend. Two, my sister was my other best friend. Both of my siblings, though odd as it may seem to people who do not have children with special needs in their families, were my very best friends. Noe did not communicate well or often. Ila had Downs. Yet I felt as though I knew and understood them more than anyone else on Earth. Above all things, I loved and wanted to protect my brother and sister, to make sure that their lives were as happy and normal as possible. How does one protect their siblings from God, though?

"Your father did not hate you, Enzo." My mother's hand landed like a butterfly's wing upon my shoulder.

"For being gay or for grandmother's love?" I asked.

"Either." She said. *"He hated himself for not knowing about you sooner so that maybe he could have his own absolution. He hated himself for being too stupid—too macho—to admit that he loved his mother and needed her affection as much as you received it."*

"Fuck him."

Mother laughed, which shocked me.

"I think he would agree." She said.

My mother slowly eased herself off of her bed in the room she had shared with Ila and shuffled gingerly towards the door. Noe was still groaning, though his volume had decreased. I felt so ashamed for terrifying him, even if that had not been my intention. My mother turned in the doorway, one hand going to the jamb to brace herself.

"Your father loved you, Enzo. And he always wanted to be your father."

209

"How do you know? You don't know what he said to me." I growled with what little strength I had left.

"He told me what he said to you. He regretted moving us here—to this place. But he mourned the loss of his humanity from what he had said to you more. And like so many things, he did not take the time he had to say so."

I stared up at her.

"So, here we are." She gestured vaguely, weakly, with her free hand. *"What do we do with this? I am dying. There is nothing that can be done about that. Soon, this family will be two. What do you do when God has chosen to take the reins away from you so that you cannot steer your own destiny, Enzo?"*

"Do you still love me? Did Dad? Grandmother? Even though I am a sinner?"

My mother gave an incredulous laugh as her arms came to fold over her chest, and she leaned against the doorjamb. Noe was silent now.

"You seem to think that love is conditional, Enzo. We did not set parameters for our love when we found out that I was pregnant with you. Nor when you were born. Or your first year, second year…God did not give you to us after a lifetime of trying with a list of conditions. Nor Noe or Ila. We loved you just as you are, every day, every year. Until our ends. We did not say to ourselves or each other: 'We will love him only if.' Enzo…regret darkened your father's soul. His inability to accept that his choices were not bad…they just turned out to be wrong…darkened his

soul. Through no fault of his own. One doesn't know when they decide to take a job whether or not it will be the best thing for them and their family. They simply have faith. But faith is the illusion of control and the assumption of truth in a world that is chaotic and full of different truths. Do not let anger and grief do the same to you."

My mother pushed away from the door.

"Never stop loving someone because they are not what other people see as perfect, Enzo. Never let your perception of what is perfect keep you from loving others."

"But—"

"Being gay is not a sin, Enzo." My mother stated firmly, her foot stomping gently against the floorboards. *"Maybe we should have spoken to you more about the things you heard in our church, explained that church, like people, is imperfect. There are a great many things, at the end of a life, one can say that they wish they had paid more notice to, that they talked about, that they clarified. At some point, though, this ceases to matter. All you can do is forgive yourself for the mistakes you have made and pray that those you have made them against are kind enough to do the same. Here we are, Enzo. Make your choice about what you will do, but either way, love, in any of its forms, is not a sin. And, even if you can't believe that right now, remember this:* Above all, love each other deeply, because love covers a multitude of sins. *I do not want to say more about this. It is not a discussion. You are gay. Your grandmother loved you. Your father loved you. Ila loved you. I love you. Noe loves you. I am dying, and I will tell you every day that I love you*

until I am done—but I will not tolerate your doubt. I can accept that what our family has endured is God's plan, but your doubt, I will not abide. To lose a child to God's plan is one thing, to lose them to doubt is another."

"Yes, Maman."

"Your brother will need you, Enzo."

"I know."

"Come." She reached a hand out to me. *"We can clean this up later. You need to eat and drink something and rest. Noe will want to sit with you."*

"Okay."

When I left the room with my mother, even though everything was already ruined, I made sure to not step on any of Ila's memories.

Life's Simple Pleasures

Peter found a bench within moments of us scaling the inadequate fencing that surrounding the side of the park we had been walking along. Obviously, more intimate with what it meant to be dangerous than I was, Peter simply sat down and extracted the packages and boxes of chocolate candies from his coat pockets. He looked perfectly at home in a park that was supposed to be closed to the public from midnight until six in the morning. I, on the other hand, kept my hands in my pockets and glanced around nervously, expecting a police officer…a security guard…someone to come tell us that we were in trouble. Maybe we would be arrested? At the very least, we would be given a scolding and told to leave immediately, or there would be consequences. Swallowing my fear and my Good Boy tendencies, I eased myself down to sit beside Peter on the bench. Not merely because I wanted to be dangerous for once, but because I had been simply existing for so many nights in succession that I had forgotten what it meant to live.

Settling in beside Peter on the bench, making sure that the side of my leg touched his, and glad that he did not mind in the slightest, I watched as he held the candies out to me in one hand, one box of Smarties and a bag of M&Ms. Smiling, I reached out and took them from him, making sure that my hand lingered against his for as long as possible. Peter made sure his fingers brushed along mine, the tips of our fingers dancing as he transferred the candies to my hand, his eyes never leaving mine. It's a funny thing, being a virgin and having intimate contact with another human being, the things one finds to be erotic when they have no concept of what "erotic" really means. Having no experience with sex, so many things, such slight, innocent touches could electrify one's body. I found that just having the tips of my fingers play along the tips of Peter's fingers affected my body in ways that nothing else ever did.

Of course, it could have been Peter more than the thought of sex itself that did this to me. It was possible that had there been a different man sitting next to me, the sensation of fingers against fingers would have been clinical and uninspiring. Just one person passing candy to another person, no undertone of danger and sensuality. As it were, I knew, without asking, that if I had asked Peter to hold my hand or lay his on my thigh, to touch me anywhere on my body, he would have obliged. If I had asked him to kiss me, his lips would have found mine. I could have asked anything of Peter in that moment, and he would have granted my wish. Not just because he felt obligated, but because he wanted those things as much as I thought I did. He was merely waiting for my acquiescence. He wanted to know that I wanted those things as badly as he did, but he was letting me lead. There is nothing worse than feeling someone has been honest with you about their attraction, yet being rejected when you take them at their word.

We were performing a dance. Our desires clear and omnipresent, but both participants afraid to take the next step unless the other person led. It was frustrating and infuriating, nearly pushing me to the brink of anger. It was the most satisfying type of foreplay.

"So," Peter began, obviously unaware of the battle going on in my brain, "are Smarties actually good, or were you teasing me, just to trick me into trying them?"

I chuckled.

"Non," I said. "They are good. My brother used—"

Peter just watched me, waiting for me to finish a sentence I hadn't even planned to begin.

"They are good," I said finally, looking down at the packages of candy in my hand.

"Enzo?"

"I do not want to talk about that."

"Okay."

So, in silence, both of us opened candy packages. I decided to eat my M&Ms first, though I really wanted to save both to take home. I could portion them out as treats for the following few days, but I knew that it would be rude to do such a thing since Peter had purchased them for us to enjoy during our night together. Using the tips of my fingers like a pincher, I reached into my bag of M&Ms and extracted a candy, then delicately deposited it on the tip of my tongue and savored the feeling of it rolling into my mouth. It had been many months since I had experienced the luxury of candy-coated chocolate rolling around in my mouth. The candy rolling around in my mouth made me smile, not because it was delicious, though it was, but because it was such a simple thing to think of as a luxury. The sheer amount of the candies that would be consumed in a day in one city alone was astronomical, and I felt as though I was eating edible gold.

Peter was silent, other than the sound of the candies being poured into the palm of his hand and then tossed into his mouth. He stared out at nothing in the park as he sat beside me, the sides of our legs touching and candies were eaten. Guilt, but not of the Catholic kind, flooded my chest as I chewed my candy slowly, considering whether or not I had been rude to someone who had shown me nothing but kindness all evening. Had it been wrong of me to refuse to talk about Noe with Peter? Or was that within my right to decline to speak about something that was still like an open wound on my heart that I was certain would never heal—especially if I kept picking at it? Then again, did I want a wound, which was really the memories of people I loved, to become scabbed over, turning into yet another ugly scar?

"My brother was named Noe," I said finally, though my voice was weak as I stared out at the same nothing as Peter. "He liked Smarties. Actually, I think he just liked sugar."

"Was he younger than you?"

"Yes."

"Most young kids love sugar."

I nodded slowly, another candy finding its way into my mouth as I stared ahead blankly.

"He had very few pleasures in life," I added. "Life was—it was harsh? For him."

A pause. A pregnant uncertainty of whether or not questions should be asked.

"Why?"

"He was autistic. And black." I said, simply. "I suppose what I mean to say is that life was not harsh but that people made it harsh for him. The world is full of people who would think nothing of being cruel to him."

"Candy was one of life's simple pleasures."

"Yes," I said, my eyes finally coming back into focus as I turned to look at Peter. He turned his body so that his knee slid up onto the bench between us, but he made sure that we still touched. "And when I could not provide that simple pleasure was when I always felt the worst."

Peter did not answer, but I could tell he understood.

"Noe was my best friend."

That was all I had left to say that I felt I could say without falling apart. Another candy was deposited into my mouth.

"When did he…?"

"A few months ago."

"I see."

"Yes."

Again, we sat in a pregnant silence as we stared at each other, but not really seeing each other. Both of us were looking at something that wasn't there.

"Can I have your candy?" Peter held his hand out expectantly.

Without thinking, I held the mostly full bag of M&Ms out to Peter. He took them from me and then moved closer.

"Open up." He smiled.

"What?"

"Open your mouth." Peter shook the bag of candies at me mischievously. "You are eating them wrong if you are trying to honor Noe. I think he would shove as many into his mouth as he could at one time."

"No. Well, yes." I couldn't help but laugh. "But I am not doing that."

"Why?" Peter pretended to be aghast. "Are you trying to just exist again?"

I frowned at him, though I was not unamused.

"Don't you think Noe would want you to shove as many M&Ms in your mouth as you could at one time?"

"Is this a naughty talent thing?"

Peter brayed with laughter as I grinned at him.

"Don't make this dirty." Peter admonished me playfully once he got himself under control. "This is about Noe. I think you need to eat a huge mouthful of sugar to honor him. Don't just eat them one by one. Stuff your face full and do your best to chew them all up without letting them spill out of your mouth. Be crazy, Enzo. Stop just existing."

For a moment, I considered Peter's suggestion. How happy would Noe be to see me shoving that many candies in my mouth at one time, savoring the overabundance of sugar?

"Don't make fun of me," I warned him.

"Never." Peter moved his hand that held the M&Ms closer.

"And don't do anything weird."

"What's weird?" He asked, evilly.

I laughed, then before I could question anything, I tilted my head back and opened my mouth widely to receive the candies. Peter brought the bag to my mouth and poured them, slowly at first, then practically dumped them into my mouth. I started to sputter with laughter as the hard, little bites of candy-coated chocolate filled my mouth, threatening to fill my mouth to the brim and spill over. Most of the candies stayed in my mouth as the bag was finally emptied, and I tilted my head back up, closing my mouth quickly, my cheeks bulging. Peter laughed as my eyes bugged, and I did my best to chew all of the candies. Peter laughed, not at my difficulties in chewing the candies, but in the joyous absurdity of it all, as I continued to struggle to keep the candies in my mouth and chew.

"This is living, Enzo." He proclaimed as I choked down the first bit of semi-chewed candies. "Sitting in a closed park after midnight with a mouthful of M&Ms."

All I could do was try to indicate that I agreed with my eyes because even something such as attempting to smile would have caused candies to spill from my mouth. Peter laughed, and I chewed and swallowed, and together we celebrated Noe's love of sugar. Just as the last bit of candies were getting crushed between my teeth and swallowed down, a bitter gust of wind whipped through the park, slashing against our cheeks and blowing the M&Ms wrapper from Peter's hand. I choked down the rest of the candy with a grimace as Peter and I watched the empty wrapper flutter upwards and away from us. My eyes followed the dark brown wrapper, black in the stark, cold darkness of night, as it fluttered through the air and got snagged in a tree branch above our heads.

"Shit," Peter said. "We've left evidence of our crime, Enzo. We're going to have to go on the lam or end up in prison."

I chuckled as I stared up at the wrapper.

"We cannot leave evidence." I shook my head playfully. "I do not want to go to prison. But mostly, I do not want to seem like an amateur criminal."

"It belongs to the tree now." Peter shrugged comically. "All we can do is accept our fate."

"I can get it."

"You're tall." Peter chuckled. "But there's no way you can reach that."

"Maybe if I run and jump—"

"No way." Peter scoffed, drawing my eyes back to him.

"How dare you?" I feigned offense.

"How dare I?" Peter waggled his head haughtily. "How dare you embellish your abilities merely to impress me?"

"Embellish?" I couldn't help but smile at the absurdity of our conversation. "I can reach it."

"Liar."

"How rude."

"Prove it."

"I will."

"Do it," Peter said.

"I will."

"What are you waiting for, huh?"

"A good reason."

"Fine." Peter held a finger to his chin thoughtfully. "For your efforts in retrieving the evidence which would surely land us in prison—if not an execution date—I will give you a kiss."

Immediately, I blushed, and my chin dipped to my chest again, a smile coming to my face against my will. Peter coughed slightly, obviously also astounded at his forwardness.

"I mean...ya' know...if that is an acceptable prize."

Nothing I could think to say would make me seem adequately cool enough in my own eyes, so I merely looked up, my cheeks surely still rosy, and nodded.

"I can do it."

"I hope you can," Peter stated hoarsely.

Slowly, I rose from the bench, my eyes still on Peter's, and held my unopened box of Smarties out to him, which he eagerly took from my hand, though I could tell he was trying not to seem eager. My fingers went to the buttons on the front of my new coat, and I stared into Peter's eyes as I undid each button methodically, then pushed it off of my shoulders. Peter's Adam's Apple bobbed in his throat as I pulled the coat off and handed it to him without a word. He took the coat in his hand and held it close as I stared at him. Without a word still, I began backing up, my eyes never leaving Peter's. After several backward strides, I pried my eyes from Peter's and looked up at the wrapper, still snared by the tree limb overhead. My body rocked on the balls of my feet a few times, preparing to run and jump for the wrapper.

A kiss from Peter.

I thought it once, and my feet propelled me forward without my willing it, and I was running full speed towards the bench. When I was almost under the tree limb, I pushed off of the ground and leapt, my hand reaching out for the wrapper. My eyes shut, and I felt a wish enter my mind at the same time I thought of a kiss from Peter once more. My fingers found their prize and wrapped around the empty wrapper, yanking it free from the tree limb. I nearly stumbled, falling into Peter and the bench, but even though I corrected my stance and caught myself, I found that I wouldn't have cared if my landing had been imperfect. The prize I desperately wanted would be mine…though I was suddenly overcome with dread at the thought of collecting it.

What if I am a bad kisser?

I've never kissed anyone before.

Not like that.

"Holy shit." Peter was grinning widely when I opened my eyes. "You actually got it."

"I told you I would," I said, simply.

"I should have known better than to assume you would lie about…anything."

I shrugged, my cheeks flushed.

"My hero." Peter batted his eyelashes at me, making me chuckle nervously. "I suppose fair is fair."

Peter stood from the bench, my coat still in his hand.

"What?"

"I have to kiss you now, don't I?"

"You do not have to." *What the hell was I saying?* "It was just a silly bet."

"You proved you aren't a liar," Peter said. "I have to prove that I'm not either."

"Well," I said, searching for some way to avoid a kiss I so desperately wanted but was terrified to receive, "maybe I do not want to seem easy?"

"You don't want a kiss from me?" Peter held a hand to his chest, though his cheeks betrayed his playful action.

"I don't know now." I tilted my nose up in the air, though my cheeks were surely betraying me. "How do I know it is a worthy prize?"

"You little shit." Peter laughed loudly. "Now you're definitely getting a kiss."

Like a child, I squealed gleefully as Peter jumped towards me, and I jumped out of his way with a laugh, running away, but not putting any real effort into it. Peter chased after me, my coat flapping in his hand as I held tightly to the M&Ms wrapper and ran around the park bench. For several moments, Peter chased me around the park bench, trying to catch me so that he could give me the kiss he had promised when we had made our bet. If I had wanted, I could have easily outrun Peter in our little game, but I was not trying to outrun him. I was simply teasing him, while also trying to figure out if I had the courage to accept the kiss I so desperately wanted. Peter laughed and chased me, trying just hard enough to catch up, but giving me enough leeway so that if I was caught and given a kiss, it was because I wanted it to happen.

Laughing as I rounded the back of the bench for what seemed like the hundredth time, I cut to my right and leapt the bench like it was an Olympic hurdle. Peter, having seen me telegraph my actions, turned around and started running towards the front of the bench, and we collided. Laughing and grasping at each other so that we didn't tumble to the ground, I found Peter's arms around my middle as mine went around his shoulders. Heaving breaths and laughing, Peter's forehead met my chin as he leaned into me, trying to catch his breath. Breathing heavily, I held onto him, laughing and doing my best not bury my nose in his ginger waves of hair to see if he smelled as amazing as he looked. As we caught our breath and held each other, Peter's head tilted back so that he could look up at me, and I felt his hot breath at the front of my throat.

Our eyes locked, and our laughing tapered off, though our heavy breathing somehow did not abate. Peter's eyes searched mine as he breathed against my throat, and I felt him rise to his tiptoes, his mouth attempting to meet mine. I swallowed hard as Peter stared into my eyes, and I breathed against his mouth, needing to do nothing more than move forward mere inches so that my lips could connect with his. But I couldn't force myself to do it. Instead, we stared into each other's eyes and breath against each other's mouths for what seemed like an eternity, though it was probably only a few seconds. Finally, Peter lowered himself to stand flat on his feet, and he cleared his throat, looking shaky as he caught his breath.

"You should…we should probably get this back on you." He said, raising my jacket to slowly pull it around me. "You'll get cold."

I breathed out shakily.

"Yes."

Peter draped my jacket around me, allowing me to slide my arms back into the warm sleeves, and he pulled it tightly shut around me. For the second time in the evening, his nimble fingers expertly buttoned it along the length of my torso. Finally, he gave the front of the jacket a tug, as if testing it to make sure that it was securely buttoned before looking up into my eyes once more. Without another word, we both turned toward the bench, as though we had choreographed this moment, and sat down next to each other once again. Sitting there for a moment, both of us finally caught our breath, and we settled into a tense but comfortable silence again. Peter reached into the pocket of his jacket and extracted a box of Smarties, then held them out to me. I reached over and took them from him, my fingertips playing along his once more, electrifying and thrilling.

In silence, we began eating candy again.

I could have kissed Peter.

I knew that was my call to make.

Peter was going to let me make the decision of how my first kiss would go.

However, I could suffer the indignity of kissing him and finding out that I was a bad kisser. I could not suffer the indignity of kissing someone I knew that I would never see again once our night together was over.

Quicker Is Better

It was a warm, early summer morning when my mother decided that she didn't want to take any more of her medications. Things were going well for her as far as managing her pain level, and she did not seem to be affected by the side effects of her cancer as much as she once was. She had come to me on the morning she decided to stop taking her pills—a day when I would have gone to the pharmacy to spend money we did not have to refill her prescriptions—and told me that the money would be better spent elsewhere. It was early summer, but fall and winter always arrive year after year, and Noe would need a new coat. His old coat was so threadbare that it would not get him through the beginning of fall. She told me that I should take the money for her medications and go to the store with Noe to find him a coat so that he would be comfortable for the coming months.

Though we both pretended that this was wonderful news, the feeling that she did not need to take her medications anymore, we both knew this to be a lie. As I looked into my mother's eyes, listening to her suggest that we use the money for a coat for Noe, I smiled and nodded. Yes. This was wonderful news. You are getting better, and the medication is unnecessary now. This was the lie we told each other with our eyes. Regardless of what tales we told with our body language, we both knew the truth. These were the final days for my mother. The calm before the storm. It wasn't that she didn't need her medication anymore; it was simply that the medications were pointless. She would probably feel well for a few weeks…and then things would change. And she would never recover. Seeing Noe with a new coat, prepared for the coming winter, would make that last descent more bearable for her.

So, I did not question her decision. I smiled, nodded, shared a lie with my eyes, and promised that I would find Noe a reasonably priced coat with this little extra money that we now had. Noe and I got dressed that morning, prepared to go to a thrift store, and search high and low for a nice coat that would serve its purpose. Hopefully, for a few years. Maman said that she would nap while we were out, reluctant to leave the apartment for long when she was never sure how long she would feel well enough to be on her feet. When Noe and I left our apartment, walking the few blocks to the nearest thrift store, my hand on his forearm to make sure that he was safe, though he was well into his teenage years then, I was able to forget my mother's condition. I didn't have to think about what had happened and what was to come for my family. Noe and I had a mission.

When we got to the thrift store, nearly empty at such an hour on a weekday, which was fortunate for Noe and his aversion to crowds, I felt hopeful. Maybe I was being overly optimistic after Maman, and I had convinced ourselves that she was getting better. Maybe I knew that I was lying to myself that our little family that was now only three would somehow find a way to flourish after our years of poor luck. Or maybe I just knew that there had been so many bad days behind us that I would lie about that day being a good day no matter what we encountered when we set out from our apartment on foot. The universe was going to smile down upon us, if only for an hour while we searched out a decent secondhand coat.

"*It smells funny in here,*" Noe said upon entering the store, his eyes on the ground.

"*I know, mon petit monstre.*" I chuckled, letting my hand slide from his forearm. "*But we won't stay any longer than we have to.*"

Mon petit monstre? Noe was always nearly as tall as me.

"*Do you promise?*"

"*I promise.*"

"*I don't want a coat that smells like this place, Enzo.*"

"*I will wash it as many times as I need to so that it smells nice for you, Noe,*" I reassured him. "*You won't have to wear it until it is clean. I promise.*"

"*Okay.*"

"*What color are we looking for?*" I asked though I knew the answer.

"*Blue,*" Noe answered automatically. "*I like blue, Enzo.*"

"*Then we will have to find a blue coat.*" I smiled, leading my brother further into the store. "*We won't stop looking until we find a blue coat.*"

"*Okay. But I don't want to stay in here forever. I don't like it in here.*"

"*Then we have to see quicker than we've ever seen before.*"

"*That's dumb.*" Noe laughed. "*People do not see quickly.*"

"*I see quickly,*" I responded impishly. "*Do not doubt the powers of your brother, monstre.*"

"*Okay. You see quickly, I guess.*"

"*Exactly. How quickly do you think I can see this new coat?*"

Noe turned his head to look at me, his eyes landing on my chin.

"*Seven minutes.*" He said. "*I want you to find it in seven minutes.*"

"*What if I am quicker than that?*"

"*Quicker is better.*"

Smiling, I gave him a nod. Together, we ventured deeper into the thrift shop, my eyes scanning the room for any hint of blue. Hoping against hope, I knew that finding a blue jacket that fit Noe's frame that he would actually like would be a miracle. Noe was particular—at least that was how most people would say it—but I knew that my brother simply liked the things he liked and disliked the things he disliked. He never tried to be difficult; he just presented unique challenges that were different than those posed by people who were not autistic. Regardless of his requirements for a coat, I did my best to stay optimistic and hopeful as we walked through the shop, Noe either at my side or a breath's space behind me.

When we were in public, where strange people or a crowd might affect him in a way that was not ideal, Noe stayed nearby. He had trained himself—with no direction from me—to stay at my side so that if he felt overwhelmed, he could grab onto me for comfort. Never my hand. Hands were not to be touched. But he could grab my shoulder or forearm, or even just place his hand against my back, and he felt calmer. Those touches let him know that he had someone who would advocate for his safety and comfort no matter the circumstances.

Walking through the thrift shop, I was glad that we seemed to be the only customers. Not because I didn't want Noe holding onto me for support, that didn't bother me in the slightest, no matter what looks we got from strangers. Not having to worry about Noe becoming anxious made me happy because he could just be Noe. Anytime that Noe didn't have to worry about what the next challenge presented to him would be made my heart soar. People without autism—or other unique challenges—took for granted the simple pleasure of merely walking through a store, looking for a blue coat, and not becoming overwhelmed by stimuli. Not having strangers in the store meant that Noe could simply live and focus solely on that.

"*It smells worse,*" Noe said as we walked deeper into the store.

"*I think that many of these clothes have not been washed well.*"

"*I know.*"

"*Do you want—*"

Suggesting that maybe I take Noe home so that he could relax and I could come back to the thrift shop alone to search for a coat had been the first idea that popped into my mind. It wasn't the best idea, as it was a risk to purchase a coat without Noe's approval first, but I didn't want him to become distressed by the smell of the store, which was, admittedly, pungent. However, before the entire thought could travel from my brain and off of my tongue, a flash of sky-blue caught my eye. Turning to the clothing rack to my right, I immediately knew I had found what we were looking for in the shop.

"*Look,*" I said to Noe, pointing at the coat.

Noe turned and found the sky-blue coat immediately, with its puffy sleeves and panels. It was like a giant marshmallow. Except it was blue. Without asking, I could tell from Noe's face that he was enamored with the idea of the coat immediately.

"*It's a good blue.*" He said simply.

I pulled the coat off of the hanger it was dangling from and held it up against my chest. It was a little too big for me, but it would work perfectly for Noe, who was always thicker in the torso than I.

"*Do you want to try it on?*"

"*I want you to wash it first.*"

That was Noe's way of saying that this was the perfect coat, and he wanted to wear it as soon as it was clean enough to do so.

"*Are you sure? We can look to see if there is something you like better.*"

"*It's a pretty blue.*"

"*All right.*" The coat was perfect, and that was all there was to say about it.

It took some doing, finding the person actually running the shop—she had been in the back alley having a cigarette and not paying attention to the store for some reason—but we finally purchased the coat. She gave it to us for five dollars. Noe was ecstatic—in his own way—and I was thrilled that we had spent a mere tenth of the money in my pocket. As we left the store, Noe carrying the bag containing his new coat, my heart felt full. Feeling immense happiness from simply finding a cheap, decent coat for Noe made the previous months and years fade away for the briefest of moments. So, when we stepped out into the warm breeze of summer in the city, I was able to merely exist. Instead of survive.

"It looks like a cloud."

Noe didn't have to tell me he was talking about his coat.

"A blue cloud," I responded with a smile.

"Clouds aren't blue." He gave an incredulous laugh.

"They aren't, are they?" I laughed with him. *"We have money left over. Do you want to go get some donuts?"*

"Can we take some to Maman?"

"Absolutely. I think we will take the bus. Is that okay?"

"Okay."

So, Noe and I had a coat made of blue clouds. And we got an entire box of donuts, along with a few to take home to our maman. We rode the bus there and back to our apartment. It was a good day. The best we'd had in…I couldn't remember. A coat made of blue clouds that cost five dollars had given us the best day we'd had as a family in a very long time. When we got home, Noe showed Maman his coat and explained how I had found it in less than seven minutes. Then, when Noe had left Maman's room to put his coat in the kitchen for me to wash, I presented the donuts we had brought for her. I explained that we had only spent five dollars on the coat, so we spent some more on donuts and the bus, hoping that she would not be cross with me for making those financial decisions on my own.

She was far from cross. She was thrilled. And she ate her donuts as I sat on the edge of her bed and talked to her about how well she was feeling, even though she was still tired after her nap.

When my father had died, it seemed sudden. Maybe because of what he had said to me and the fact that we never made amends while he was able to speak. When my mother died, a month after we found Noe's coat made of blue clouds, it seemed slow. Maybe because the process was torturous for her, the dying. She didn't go to sleep and not wake up like my grandmother or Ila after her surgery. She didn't fall sick one day and die the next. Incrementally, over the days in her final month, she got sicker, frailer, and suffered through it all. She didn't live in that final month. She slowly died.

The thing is, no matter how sudden or gradual a family member's death is, there never seems to be enough time to say: "Goodbye."

But, then again, how does one say "goodbye" to a person who loves you, sins and all?

Fury

"*No one would want your brother anyway. No one wants a black autistic teenager as a permanent ward. You may as well be his guardian until we can figure something out. He will be an adult in a few years. Just keep him out of trouble as best you can. They're going to cut off your assistance. You're an adult, white male. Noe has no real legal guardian. It will be difficult to approve assistance in your case. Maybe if you were real brothers—*"

Noe had been sitting next to me the entire time.

And I wasn't allowed to show my fury.

Because then I never would have seen my brother again.

Even more so than dealing with the death of your family members, one by one, choosing between defending your brother and being able to see him every day is the greatest torture one can endure.

Fury, like any other emotion, demands to be shown. But, unlike other emotions, fury is the one that most often leads to trouble. And a choice has to be made. I had to make a choice I didn't agree with, but was safest, for what was left of our little family.

A soul is permanently fractured by such a thing.

And nothing will ever fix it.

A Lifetime of Perfect Sundays

"We have to be very quiet," I whispered as we sat on the edge of the fountain in Carré Saint-Louis. "We do not want anyone to call the police."

Gesturing vaguely at the Victorian and Second Empire homes that surrounded St. Louis Square as Peter eased himself down beside me, I knew that we could easily get in trouble. Someone could phone in a noise disturbance or say we were vagrants. They could easily convince the police that we were vandals. Regardless of Peter's belief that the police would be more lenient with an American tourist, he was wrong. The police would gladly arrest an American tourist they suspected of disrespecting one of the city's famous landmarks.

"Of course not." Peter leaned in and wriggled his eyebrows at me. "There is nothing worse than handcuffs on a first date—if police are involved, anyway."

"You are awful." I cupped a hand over my mouth to keep from laughing.

"I'm not nearly as awful as I make myself out to be." Peter shrugged, an impish grin on his face. "I talk a big game, but I am really quite sweet."

"In general—or in the bedroom?"

"Well, in general." He agreed, keeping his voice low as well. "In the bedroom…well, it depends on who I am with."

"What—what if it was with me?" I was emboldened to ask, feeling safe in the quiet and stillness of the square and the beautiful homes that surrounded us.

Peter considered me for a long time, which should have made me feel self-conscious, but it didn't. Something about Peter made me feel as if, when he looked at me, he was really considering his answers to my questions, as though he took everything I asked seriously. It made me feel important. Not in the way that causes arrogance or delusions of grandeur. It was in the way that someone who cares about you makes you feel important. Just to them.

"I feel that with you," Peter replied evenly, "I would be happy with whatever you were happy with."

I blushed.

"Though I'm sure you are not always sweet." He leaned to bump his shoulder against mine.

"I wouldn't know."

"Everyone *knows*, Enzo." Peter was grinning again. "Even if you've never had sex, you have an image in your mind of how you would like things to go once you do it."

"I suppose."

"So," Peter prodded me, "do you think you're always sweet?"

"Stop it." I chuckled nervously.

"Not until you answer me."

"No." I sighed, pretending to be put out. "I would not be sweet always."

Peter's grin grew.

"Stop it."

"Okay." He couldn't stop grinning.

So, I grinned with him.

"It's very quiet here," Peter said, mercifully changing the subject.

"Yes." I agreed, clearing my throat as quietly as possible. "It is one of my favorite places in the city. When it is not full of people."

"What's with all of the houses?" Peter asked as he leaned to reach into his pocket, extracting his cigarettes. "I mean…they're nice, though."

"It is very European, yes?" I asked, taking a cigarette from Peter's pack when he offered one.

"You would know better than me." He lit his cigarette and then held the lighter out, a cupped hand around it so that I could light my own. "But, yeah, I would agree. It looks very European, anyway."

"It is." I pulled in a lungful of smoke and blew it out, blue and fragrant into the dark night and crisp autumn air. "I would love to live in one of these houses. Wake up each morning and open my curtains and look out onto the square."

"Yeah?"

"Yes." I nodded slowly, my eyes scanning the houses. "Obviously, with my partner. We would kiss each other good morning and then sit at the window in our bedroom and eat breakfast and drink coffee on a Sunday morning. And we would talk."

"What would you talk about?" Peter's voice sounded dreamy.

"Life. Art. Books. Politics. How much we love our life together."

"Then what?" Peter was leaning in, his eyes far away.

"Then," I chewed at my lip with a grin, "maybe we would be not so sweet. Or maybe sweet. Whatever our mood was that day."

Peter sighed, shaking his head, his eyes looking clearer.

"That sounds like a nice Sunday."

I sat up straight, bringing my cigarette to my lips.

"Then," I took a puff of my cigarette and blew it out quickly, turning to face Peter, "we would walk to the market and find the perfect food for dinner. Which we would cook together while music played and we danced slowly in the kitchen. And we would eat together at the table and talk more. Maybe we would have a dog who would be begging for scraps."

Peter chuckled.

"That sounds amazing."

"And we would not let the world intrude upon our life for that day." I declared. "Every Sunday would be like that."

"I would love your Sundays."

"We are very stupid." I sighed, the cigarette coming to my lips.

"Are we?" Peter frowned. "Why?"

"We do not really know each other at all," I replied. "We are like teenagers. Our eyes have stars in them, and we will only know each other for tonight."

"Do you want to love Sundays with me or not?" Peter ignored me.

"That is a pointless question." I shrugged. "I—"

Suddenly, Peter leapt up from his seated position on the fountain wall, coming to stand upright upon it. He held his arms out wide, gesturing grandly at the neighborhood that surrounded us.

"Pick a house, Enzo!" He declared loudly. "Tell me which is your favorite, and I will make it yours! I will buy you your castle, and we will rule over our dominion together! Every Sunday will be ours to drink coffee and be not so sweet and cook dinners together! Anything you wish, I will make it my life's work to make it happen for you! I am your servant!"

"You have gone mad." I gasped, though a laugh escaped my throat. "Sit down. We will get in trouble."

"No! I refuse!" Peter stated in a manner that you usually would expect from a drunk person, though I supposed he was drunk in a way. "I will not sit down until you tell me which house will become your castle! I will not rest until every dream of yours comes true! Until you allow me to make your dreams come true! Grant me the honor of making your dreams come true!"

Quickly, I reached up and pulled Peter down until he was seated beside me again. I was stifling my laughter as I glanced around, making sure none of the houses' porch lights were flickering to life. Peter was calmly smoking his cigarette when I turned to him again. A dog was barking in one of the distant yards.

"You are insane."

"You caused it."

"Me?" I gasped. "How is your madness my fault?"

"You said asking you if you wanted to spend Sundays with me was pointless," Peter explained calmly. "I could not abide that."

"Yes, but—"

"Would you want to spend your perfect Sundays with me or not?" Peter asked.

"Peter, that is—"

He started to stand again. I grabbed his arm, holding him back.

"I would want to spend perfect Sundays with you," I said urgently. "Sundays with you would be wonderful. I would want to spend a lifetime of perfect Sundays with you. Is that what you want to hear?"

"If that's what you want to say."

"It is."

Peter nodded and settled back on the edge of the fountain, bringing his cigarette to his lips with a grand gesture.

"You are happy with yourself?" I rolled my eyes, though a smile came to my face.

"Immensely."

"Good."

"So, which house?" He asked.

"Could you really buy one of these houses?"

"Of course, not." He chuckled. "They probably want millions of dollars for the smallest one. But if I could, I would do that for you. However, we can pretend."

Nodding slowly, I scanned the neighborhood. Finally, I found my answer.

"I would want the smallest one," I answered. "As long as you are in it."

Peter turned his head to me, a shy smile pulling at the corners of his mouth.

"I've never heard a more perfect answer to a question."

"This is stupid."

"You said that before. But is it?"

"Yes. Well, no. I do not know."

"I don't think it is," Peter said. "If you lived in the U.S.—"

"But, I do not."

"—I would take you on dates." Peter continued, ignoring me. "I would woo you in every way that you deserved to be wooed."

"Woo?"

"It's not sexual like it sounds. It's very sweet." He replied, then continued. "And I would make you realize that living is so much better than existing. And I would let you turn my house into your castle. I would love having a relationship with you—even though I would have to do my part to keep that relationship strong."

"You do not know me."

"I think I do."

"Why are you so sure?"

"Because you're trying to convince a really awesome guy like me that you are not worth my time." Peter grinned wickedly. "Only someone who wants nothing but someone to love would convince a great guy to have nothing to do with them."

Love.

No one had ever said that word with a tinge of possibility to me before.

No man had ever suggested that maybe one day they would love me and I would love them.

"You are great?" I teased, pushing that word to the corner of my mind.

"Amazing."

"How do I know that you are not lying to me?"

"Why would I lie to you?" Peter countered. "If we will only know each other for tonight, what purpose would lying to you serve?"

"Maybe you are crazy?"

"Undoubtedly."

"Maybe you are a narcissist."

"I have my moments."

"Maybe you are just trying to get me into bed."

"Eventually."

"You are crazy."

"You love it."

"I thought that I was too young for you?" I asked. "Or, you are too old for me?"

"You make me feel young."

"You do not make me feel old."

"Told you I was amazing."

"Then what do we do now?" I shrugged. "The sun will be up soon. And you are leaving for America."

Peter stared at me.

"Our castle is…is…crumbling?"

"How can something we are planning to build crumble before we build it?"

"Where will we build it?"

"America," Peter answered quickly. "We will have our castle in America."

"Why not Québec?"

"You hate Québec."

"I don't hate it. It is just—just—"

"Say it." Peter wiggled his eyebrows at me. "Say you hate Québec. I want to hear you say it."

"Why?"

"It turns me on."

"You really are crazy."

"Surely."

"I hate Québec."

"Yes." Peter moaned comically.

I chuckled.

"But I do not." I shook my head with a sigh. "Québec is…if things were different, Québec would be…nice."

"So, maybe you hate what Québec represents?"

"Maybe."

"Minneapolis is nice," Peter said lowly. "I think you would like Minneapolis."

"Are you going to put me in your suitcase?" I teased, leaning down to stub my cigarette out on the ground.

Peter followed my lead.

"Now *that* is insane," Peter responded. "You would ride in an airplane seat like anyone else."

I had no response to that suggestion.

"You will fly to America, and I will woo you." Peter nodded. "And you will see that I was not lying about being an amazing guy. And then you will want to build your castle with me."

"I am Québécois." I said, simply. "I am not American citizen. I would not be allowed to stay for long, especially for as long as it takes to build a castle."

"You are not Québécois." Peter shook his head. "You are a citizen of the world, Enzo. I know that about you. You have never felt like you belonged anywhere you have lived, so every place is the same. So…why not Minneapolis? Maybe you will feel like you belong there."

"You are completely insane."

"You keep saying that." Peter was grinning yet again. "But you haven't once told me to stop talking. You haven't said I'm wrong."

"So?"

"Sunrise is coming."

"Yes."

"Confessing the truth is easier in the dark of night."

"Why?"

"Because the night knows us in ways that the day never will. We have a primal, evolutionary fear of the dark and unknown. The truth isn't as scary when it's stood next to that."

"That is—"

"Insane?"

"Yes."

"So? What's the truth?"

"I don't know you."

"Are you really so sure?"

"No. But maybe I need to know more."

"Ask me anything."

"What is your favorite color?"

"Red. Specifically, the color of red some Maple leaves turn in Fall." Peter answered quickly. "My favorite food is anything I am not supposed to eat and lots of it. My favorite movie is books. I sleep on the left side of the bed, even now that I am single, instead of sleeping in the middle, because I am saving room and hope. I love red wine and dark beer. And sometimes I overdo it. I never go to church unless someone I like and care about invites me. Dogs are better than cats. My job is boring, but I love it. I never thought about having kids because I would make a poor father, though my parents are great. When I was a kid, I thought I'd be a movie star because I liked being the center of attention, though I despise it now. And when I wake up on Sundays at home, and I have no one to share coffee with or be not so sweet with, sometimes I feel like crying."

Again, I was unsure of what, if anything, I could say.

"Lastly, I know without a doubt that two people do not have a night like this unless pieces of them knew each other when stars exploded billions of years ago. Call that God or providence or the universe moving us along, but I know it to be true."

"You are—"

"Insane?"

"Wonderful," I whispered. "I was going to say 'wonderful.'"

"Thank you."

"I am not so sure the universe is on my side anymore."

"That's between you and the universe." Peter shrugged. "But it's just you and me right now. Even if the universe is listening in."

"How do I know that you are not just saying these things because you will never see me again?"

"I will see you again, Enzo." Peter leveled me with his eyes. "And when I do, I won't let you go. I know this is insane, and you think I'm mad—hell, maybe I am—but, well, here we are."

"What?" I was suddenly finding it hard to breathe.

"Here we are." Peter shrugged. "What do we do with this?"

My chest began to heave as I fought to breathe, and I leapt up from the side of the fountain. Before I could stop myself, I was running away as Peter screamed for me to stop.

Where A Heart Belongs

C hristmas was always my favorite time of year. Even though my mother was adamant that we attend church services for Midnight Mass on Christmas Eve and then services again on Christmas morning, making those two days very sleepy days, I still loved Christmas. Réveillon on Christmas Eve with the oyster stew—which I picked the oysters out of—escargot (which I pushed around my plate), the duck and scallops, roasted vegetables, chestnuts, sometimes caviar (which I also hated), turkey, and cheeses. The thirteen (or more) desserts, of which I had a little of each. Putting my shoes by the fireplace for Père Noël's imminent visit—when I still believed in such things. Maman would have music playing before and after dinner, right up until Midnight Mass. *Il Est Né Le Divin Enfant* always played, followed by *Douce Nuit, Sainte Nuit*. Possibly *Le Petit Renne Au Nez Rouge* if my mother was in the right mood to allow silly songs to be played. Usually, we listened to slow, traditional Christmas songs or songs with religious themes that my mother felt fit the holiday, but I loved them all. Some songs and foods, when experienced together, replay memories a person feels they have forgotten.

Growing up in my childhood home in Mantes, Christmas was a religious event—as well it should be, all things considered. It's quite literally the observance of the birthday of the son of God—though that aspect of my religion I felt difficult to truly believe. Regardless, my parents, and especially my grandmother, felt that Christmas was also about joy and thankfulness. We were not only allowed to think about our God, his son, and our religion. We were allowed to enjoy each other. To be thankful for and celebrate our home and food. As religious as my parents could be at times, especially my mother, she saw the value in appreciating what God had provided. That was my favorite thing about Christmas. That and the gifts, of course.

Gifts, even when our financial situation allowed for luxuries, were often meager in our home. My parents were not tolerant of ostentations or gross displays of wealth., though I would get at least one toy every year that was quite nice. Shoes, socks, clothing, books, anything educational, food—these were the gifts that my parents appreciated most. Père Noël's visits were something I looked forward to every year, until I grew out of it, though I always found he left me much different gifts than my friends at school. Nuts and fruit, a book, maybe some chocolates, were what he felt that I deserved year after year. Though I wasn't upset by this, I just found it odd that he treated me so differently than my friends. I vacillated between feeling special compared to my friends and less liked than my friends, based on what was left each Christmas morning.

Things changed when Noe, and then Ila, joined our family. Christmases became even more joyous. Ila always got toys and sweets, and Noe always got books about rocks and animals that contained lots of pictures. And *Le Petit Renne Au Nez Rouge* always found its way into the song rotation on Christmas Eve. Maman became laxer in what she did and didn't allow at Christmas once our family became bigger. The food changed as well. The things I hated so much—the oysters and caviar and escargot were replaced with succulent cuts of pork and beef, though the turkey and duck were still present. The desserts became more lavish and varied so that there was something everyone would eat. Ila and Noe—and their particular challenges—were a boon for a young me. I hated to think of their difficulties with certain foods as a good thing for myself, but it was simply fact. Their aversions to certain things that I simply just didn't want to eat made life easier on me. It was something I prayed about at church on every visit.

I think God understood.

Christmas was about God and family and church and the appreciation of all of those things. It was on Christmas Eve, after our prayers were said around the table, before we dug into the glorious meal my mother had made, that my father made his announcement. I was still holding grandmother's hand in one of mine and Ila's in the other, from saying the prayer, when my father got our attention. Noe had put his foot on top of mine under the dinner table like he often did for comfort.

We were going to leave France.

That's what my father had to say.

He had accepted a job offer in Canada—a place I knew quite a bit about from my studies in school, though I understood very little about it. We were going to be leaving before spring arrived. When the last of his words left his mouth, I had leapt up from our holiday table and darted for the door, running from this announcement.

I didn't get far.

I wasn't wearing appropriate shoes. I was wearing my nice black leather shoes with slick soles that my mother insisted I wear for Réveillon, along with my nice black slacks and my holiday sweater that I absolutely loathed. When the bottoms of my shoes hit the slick walkway at the bottom of the porch, my feet went over my head, and I was suddenly sitting on the concrete. Stunned, and unsure of what to do next, I simply pulled knees up to my chest and hugged them to me. I didn't want to leave France to live in a foreign country—even if I knew the languages. I didn't want to leave the life I knew and felt safe in—even if it was imperfect.

France was all I had known. Even with the racist friends and the ignorant church people and the neighbors who didn't deserve dogs and the feeling that I would never belong—it was my home. A child can learn to accept many things as long as there is familiarity to them. Mantes was awful. But it was the devil I knew.

"*Well,*" I heard my grandmother's voice coming from the porch, "*you certainly gave up quickly, didn't you? I thought I would have to chase you down the street. And I don't even have my sneakers on.*"

I lowered my head into the cavern created by my knees and arms, burying my face.

Grandmother's feet sounded on the porch steps, and then I heard her shuffling gently towards me on the front walk. Finally, she was standing beside me. I could see her legs through the gap between my thigh and my torso.

"*Are you going to sit here and freeze to death?*" She asked. "*Or are you just catching your breath before you take off running again? I need to know if I need to go put on better shoes.*"

"*You are too old to chase me.*"

She chuckled.

"*That may be so.*" She agreed. "*But I would chase you anyway. I wouldn't want you to revel in your grief alone, Enzo.*"

"*What do you know?*" I snapped, which I never did with my grandmother. "*You don't understand.*"

"*Is that a fact?*"

258

"It is."

"Do you see many people around here who look like me?"

I didn't answer. I knew I was being foolish.

"Other than down at the market or cleaning in hotels, of course."
She continued. *"I suppose that I do not understand what it means to be you, Enzo. But I understand your situation. More than anyone else in this family. So, trust me when I say that you are being unfair to your father."*

"Unfair?" I proclaimed, raising my head to glare at her.
"He is being unfair to me! I do not want to leave France, Grandmother. This is my home."

"Your family is your home, Enzo." She said. *"Not France. Wherever you have someone who loves you, you are home."*

Grumbling, I lowered my head once more, though I did not bury my face in the cavern of my body.

"I hate him."

She chuckled.

"And tomorrow the sun will still rise. Isn't that funny?"

"No. I mean…what?"

"Whether you are angry or happy or you decide to accept that this is what is to be, a new day will dawn, Enzo." She said, leaning down to place a hand on my shoulder. *"You either greet that day with a raised head, or you allow it to go on without you. Either way, it will go on."*

"I don't want to leave France, Mamie."

"*Well, I am happy here, too. But that is because I have my family. I will have my family in Canada, too.*"

"*I suppose.*"

"*And what an amazing thing.*" She sighed dreamily. "*Having such an adventure at my age. Going to live in another country halfway around the world. I have not left Mantes in…I do not know how long, Enzo. I have never been anywhere but Cambodia and France. Here we are. Who am I to see this as bad?*"

"*Mamie.*" I looked up, my eyes watery. "*What if no one likes me there either?*"

"*I will be there. I like you.*"

"*You know what I mean.*"

"*Enzo,*" She sighed and smiled down at me, "*are you telling me that you would rather lead an ordinary life simply because you are worried whether or not people will like you? I have known that you have not been happy here for quite some time. Maybe you need to have faith that Canada will bring you the happiness you want. If nothing else, at least it will be a change.*"

"*I guess.*"

"*Come inside. Be nice to your father. Apologize if you can bring yourself to do it. Then eat.*" She suggested. "*You can talk to God at church tonight.*"

"*God obviously hates me.*"

"*Then talk to the universe. Maybe it will put a good word in for you.*"

I couldn't help but laugh at that. Finally, with a sigh, I pulled myself up from the walkway, being careful as to not slip again and possibly send myself—and my grandmother—crashing to the ground once more.

"Maman will be mad that I fell in my good clothes." I grimaced as my eyes met my grandmother's. *"She will be mad that my clothes are dirty for Mass."*

"Well, lucky for you, God loves dirty behinds, too." She reached up and patted my cheek.

Of course, I had to laugh at that, too.

Grandmother took my arm in hers, under the pretense that she needed my help up the steps, though I knew she was perfectly capable.

"If you're going to chase something, Enzo, make sure there's actually something there."

"What?"

"When you ran out of the house, where were you running?"

"I don't know."

"Precisely. If you want to give chase, make sure there's something to actually chase."

"Is that why you would have chased me?"

"I would have chased you to Canada on foot if I had to, Enzo. That's how much I care."

I laughed. *"That's ridiculous. And dangerous. I mean, there is an entire ocean between here and there."*

"It's amazing, the courage one can have when they know where their heart belongs."

I never apologized to my father for dampening his good news on such a joyous night. I did wish him "Joyeux Noël" before I went to bed.

Between Enzo & the Universe

We All Want More

R unning has always been something I've excelled at from a very young age. I've rarely been the absolutely fastest runner, but I could run for miles without growing weary. When one considers how easily I trip over my own feet or bump into things when I am just walking, my exceptional running skills are even more impressive. There is something about the rhythmic pumping of my legs, my arms swinging into the air at my sides, and the wind in my hair that gives me grace and style. I'm most coordinated when I am running, but I am never at my best because running is not me. It is how I forget myself and my circumstances. It is how I clear my mind of all thoughts of what concerns me in life or the sorrows that have burrowed into my soul and refuse to vacate. I can simply run and feel the wind in my hair and the ground slamming into my feet, and all thoughts are chased away so that I do not have to face what life has presented to me.

It's an escape.

I am chasing, but I am not sure what it is I am chasing.

Peter didn't have to run far to catch me because I didn't even get to the street before I stopped running and slid to a stop in the middle of the square.

"What the hell are you doing?" Peter gasped, obviously less accustomed to quick dashes in the cold air than I. "Why are you running away?"

"I'm not," I answered stupidly. "I stopped."

"But why did you run at all?"

"You said something that reminded me of my grandmother."

"Oh."

"Yes. And my maman." I said, looking away. "I am sorry."

"Don't be sorry." Peter reached out tentatively, his hand coming to rest on my shoulder. "I didn't mean to upset you, Enzo."

"You didn't upset me." I still refused to look at him.

Not because I was upset and trying to skate around my feelings, but because I already had a tear sliding down my cheek, and I could not bear to have him see me cry twice in one night.

"Hey. Look at me, Enzo."

"No."

"Please?"

Without a single word, I turned to look at Peter, and I did nothing to hide my tears. I knew that he knew I was crying, so trying to cover my tears would have made it more obvious.

"Don't run from me."

"I wasn't running from you."

"What were you running from?"

I reached up and tapped the side of my head with a single finger.

"I hate Québec." That was all I could think to say.

"I hate Québec for you, too."

Together, we stood there, tears sliding down my face silently as we stared at each other, the chilly autumn air whistling through the square. Peter watched me for several moments, obviously unsure of what to do next, because what does one stranger do for another stranger who is crying? We had enjoyed our evening of food, jokes, flirtation, and holding each other on my bed. I had shared more with Peter than I had shared with anyone in longer than I could remember, but there was still much more to share before he truly understood anything about me. Throughout the evening, most of the secrets shared were mine, so I knew even less about Peter.

"But I would hate any city that has done to me what this city has done," I said. "It is not Québec that I truly hate."

"I know."

"I feel foolish and selfish." I reached up to scrub away my tear with the back of my coat sleeve. *My new coat*. "This is not Québec's fault, what I have been made to endure, and many people endure much worse. But I am twenty years old. And I am alone. I have never been alone, but since we arrived in this city, I have become more and more alone each year. Now…I have no one. This hurts. But…I am alive. I am standing in the center of the universe, asking it to be kind to me, or at least stop being so unkind, and I am the only person in my family it has been kind to, Peter. Does that mean I am a horrible person?"

Peter looked down.

"Who am I to demand more than what has already been given to me?" I asked, desperately. "Who am I to spend such a wonderful evening with such a wonderful person…and still want more?"

"You're just a person, Enzo." Peter looked up and shrugged. "We all want more. But what you want is not selfish. Wanting your family back and to not be alone is never selfish."

"It feels selfish." I sniffled and let out a deep breath. "I say my prayers every day, and I ask God why he has taken the people I love from me…but I have never asked why their lives were taken from them. I am awful."

"Now." Peter jabbed a finger at me. "*That* is selfish."

"What?"

"Everyone has the right to question God—to ruminate on why the universe is rarely fair," Peter explained. "The very essence of being human is to ask why, how, when, where, and how come. But debasing yourself for it is selfish. Putting yourself down, slowly beating yourself down into the ground over something so human, is selfish."

"How?"

"You're trying to deny yourself the right to grieve, Enzo." Peter shook his head, a soft smile coming to his face. "Sorrow has its right to be felt. Grief is a process. By denying yourself that process, and denying the humanity that the universe gave you, is selfish. You are being selfish with yourself."

"I suppose."

"I know so." Peter crossed his arms over his chest as he gave me a stern look. "You're denying yourself part of your journey through life and the human experience. Stop asking why things are the way they are and start asking how you will turn your life into what you want it to be. And, in the meantime, grieve the loss of your family. They deserve at least that much. Don't pray to know why, pray about how much you loved the time you had with them. What they meant to you. And pray that they know that wherever they are now. That would be the unselfish way to handle it. And stop doing it only in church, Enzo. Think about them as you do the things you used to do together. The things they loved. Think about them when you consider how happy they would be to see you thriving and moving towards something better. Think about them when you see their favorite colors or foods. Think about them when you show kindness to others that they are not here to receive from you themselves. Pray all day long that they know how happy you are. Let your prayers be your hopes and dreams, and your thanks—not your sorrow."

A sob erupted from my throat, and my chin fell to my chest.

"I just miss them so much." I managed to choke out.

"I know." Peter stepped into my body and wrapped mine up in his. "I think it might be the thing I like about you most. And it's no wonder you feel so raw about it now because when have you had a chance to otherwise? You were too busy being the healthy one."

Sobbing, I wrapped my arms around Peter, stooping slightly to bury my face in his neck, not worrying if he felt my hot tears against his flesh that would surely run rivulets down his neck, under his collar, and to flesh further down that I would love to caress with my eyes.

"I know this is crazy," Peter whispered into my ear, his lips brushing against the surface of that flesh. "Two strangers spending this evening together, professing their desires for a future together after knowing each other for mere hours. But what has the universe done to show us that this is wrong?"

"Nothing." My body shook against his as I cried.

"Exactly." He sighed. "Maybe someone has been listening to your prayers, and they hope that you were listening back, Enzo."

For several moments, I allowed myself to be held by Peter and to hold him back, but my tears finally abated, and my sobs tapered off. I felt like such an idiot.

"Are you saying that you are the answer to my prayers?" I chuckled wetly against his neck.

"Maybe." I could hear the smile in his voice. "I mean...it could be worse, ya' know."

With a sigh, I pulled back, reluctantly letting Peter go as his arms slowly slid away from me.

"You are a nice answer." I finally said.

"Ya' know what? I'll take it."

I laughed at that. I liked Peter's self-deprecation and ability to know when to not be too serious. The way that he was able to navigate conversations and my moods made me wonder if he was the perfect man—or just perfect for me. Peter was a handsome American stranger, someone who had no reason to be kind to me. However, from the moment we met, he had shown nothing but compassion, empathy, and patience for me. Certainly, it had only been hours since we had met, and almost anyone can be good for such a short amount of time, but I was not an easy person to deal with after so many years of bad luck making my moods irregular and erratic. The well of patience he possessed had to be fathoms deep, bottomless, even. If he was showing me so much kindness, I could only imagine how he treated people he knew well. That drew me to him even more.

"Are you always such a kind person?" I asked the obvious question.

"No." He sighed. "Unfortunately, though it is obviously nearly impossible to tell, I can be a real shit sometimes."

"I don't believe it."

"Well, that's another thing that's just your problem."

Laughing, I reached out and straightened his collar where my chin had crumpled it. Peter crooked his head to watch my thin fingers straighten the fabric of his shirt. As my hand pulled away, satisfied with the job done, his eyes landed on mine.

"What do you want most out of life, Enzo?"

I started to shrug but stopped myself.

"I just want to be happy."

"Well, shit." Peter cocked his head to the side. "That's easy. Come with me."

Peter held his hand out.

"What?"

"Are you going to keep asking questions, or are you going to take my hand and live, Enzo?"

"I guess…live." I chuckled and grabbed his hand.

Between Enzo & the Universe

A First and Final Christmas

My mother had been gone for months, and life had not been too bad for Noe and me, though loneliness was often a problem for both of us. It's an odd feeling, having someone, yet still feeling alone. Noe was lonely because he missed our parents, grandmother, and sister because he had loved them as deeply as I had, but also because the apartment was so silent. Noe's special challenges as a person on the spectrum had forced him to adapt to the noise that is expected with a large family. Because of that, when the noise became less and less, then was just suddenly gone, it was almost as if he hadn't just lost his family. He had lost the character of noise that had been as much a part of our family as any of the people. People on the spectrum are not incapable of adapting to situations that are challenging for them, but it is a process. Reversing that process can be even more arduous. A person on the spectrum can find ways to adapt to challenges the world presents to the point that they often don't realize they are dealing with them constantly. It just becomes a part of their routine like anything else. When those challenges are suddenly gone, it is, essentially, taking away part of their routine. The deathly silence of our apartment became a missing appendage to Noe. Combined with his grief over our dead relatives, it was almost too much for him to bear each day.

While life had not been bad, I also felt lonely. Because I had my own challenges, though I had no one to share them with anymore. Noe was comforting as a brother, but as a confidante, I could not share as much with him as I could my mother or grandmother. He did not need the extra stress of knowing that my job was barely keeping us fed with a roof over our heads. He did not need to know that getting him to school, working, taking care of our home, buying food, praying that there were no problems with him at school, and finding time to sleep with a challenging schedule was taking its toll on me. In the depth of my soul, I found myself wondering how I would deal with my challenges while also helping Noe deal with his challenges. I felt ill-equipped and knew that I was floundering.

Noe began having meltdowns at least once a day within a month after our mother's death. Things were too quiet. Things were too loud. Things were neither quiet nor loud. He didn't like the food we had. His blanket smelled funny. The kids at school were mean to him. The kids at school tried to be his friend. He didn't want friends. He felt lonely. I didn't spend enough time with him. I always hovered and invaded his space. He got enough sleep. He didn't get enough sleep. His favorite shirt wasn't clean. That was no longer his favorite shirt. The apartment was too cold. The apartment wasn't cold enough. My heart broke for my brother, and my head ached from the challenges. I had never felt so helpless and useless in my entire life.

Considering the history of my family, and all of the challenges posed over the years, I knew without a doubt that I was failing as a brother and guardian. When I had a support system, helping Noe to navigate the world around him had been challenging, but it had been doable. Without my parents, grandmother, and even Ila, I felt adrift—though I had no idea if it was a sea of uncertainty, fear, or bitterness—or a combination of the three—that I was drifting upon. I never lost my patience with Noe or became cross with him. I never lashed out or raised my voice. But, in looking back, I often wondered if that would have been preferable to slowly collapsing in on myself, losing faith in my abilities as a caregiver incrementally over days, weeks, and months.

The first Christmas without any family, besides Noe and myself, was the day that I dreaded the most. As the winter months settled in and we had no money for any lavish gifts or even Réveillon, I wondered if Noe would finally have the meltdown to end all meltdowns. I had been able to purchase enough groceries to make us heaps of pasta with chicken and vegetables, and I had purchased a rather large store-bought chocolate cake. So, on Christmas Eve, Noe sat at the kitchen table since it was the only real furniture we had left besides our beds, and read one of his books about rocks while I cooked pasta. We performed our duties as brothers and guardian and guarded in near silence, save for the sounds of boiling water, sizzling pans, and the occasional clang of metal on metal.

When dinner was ready, I brought our food to the table, and presented it to my brother, we sat down as the little family we were, thankful that we had…*something*. For the first part of the meal, we sat in silence once more, both of us eating our food, trying to savor each bite since food was usually rationed out each day to get us through each week. Once half of his food was gone, Noe finally looked up, his eyes landing on my chin, getting my attention.

"I'm sorry that I miss Maman so much." He had said.

Normally, one would respond with a speech about how a person should never be sorry for missing someone they love. But Noe wasn't sorry for missing our mother. I knew that what he meant was that he was sorry that things were so hard for both of us now. He was sorry that our situation made it harder for him to adapt to our daily challenges. And he was sorry that I was so sad all day long.

"I'm sorry I miss Maman so much, too." I had responded finally.

Noe knew that I meant that I was sorry that I wasn't more successful in making both of our lives easier on us.

"*Are we going to church after dinner?*"

"*I don't think so.*" I shook my head, looking down at my plate, suddenly no longer hungry.

"*You don't want to talk to God?*"

"*No.*"

"*Why not?*"

"*I have nothing to say to him.*"

"*I think you should talk to God.*"

"*God doesn't exist.*" My voice was hollow.

Because I didn't believe that. I had said it to spite God.

"*I still think you should talk to him,*" Noe said. "*Talking to God makes you feel better.*"

He coughed and pushed his fork into his food.

"*I wouldn't know what to say.*"

"*Tell him that you miss Maman,*" Noe suggested. "*Tell him I miss Maman, too.*"

"*You don't believe in God.*"

"*No.*"

"*Then why would you want me to tell someone you don't think exists that you miss Maman?*" I smiled slightly at Noe's skewed logic.

"*Because maybe Maman will hear it. Tell him that I miss Ila, Grandmother, and Father, too. In that order. Tell God that I miss them in that order, Enzo.*"

I nodded.

"Okay."

After dinner, I washed the dishes and put away the extra food. Then Noe and I each had a giant slice of the chocolate cake I had purchased at the store. Once we had washed our hands and faces and put on the nicest clothes we had, I zipped Noe up in his coat made of blue clouds, and we walked to church. We had to go slowly because it was not a good breathing day for Noe. Services had already begun, so we slipped into a pew towards the back, which was mostly unoccupied, and we went through the motions. Even Noe knelt when he was supposed to, stood when he was supposed to, did the prayers that he knew, crossed himself, and participated in our family's religion. I knew that he did those things, not for God, or even our family members we both desperately missed, but for me.

Once services were over, and the other *Good Catholics* filed out of the church, prepared to go home to their Christmas trees and wrapped presents and pantries full of food, Noe and I stayed behind. When the church was empty, Noe stayed in the pew while I lowered myself to the kneeler and said my prayers. But they weren't prayers. They were grievances. I told God how much I hated him for what he did to my family. And I told him that I didn't care what he thought of that. At the end, I told God that even though I hated him, would he please

279

tell Maman, Ila, Grandmother, and Father that Noe missed them and loved them.

Amen was my final word on the matter.

So, Noe got zipped back up in his coat, and I pulled my sweater tightly around myself, and we left the church to find an empty, bitterly cold street.

Noe coughed.

Between Enzo & the Universe

A Horrible, Awful, Happy Time

Peter had no reason to take me to a donut shop. Of course, donut shops are usually the first places of business that open in the early morning hours, so I knew that was the most logical explanation for him to choose such a place. However, something gnawing at the back of my mind made me wonder if maybe the universe wasn't paying attention and guiding our night together. Maybe something had whispered into Peter's ear that a donut shop would be the perfect place for me to find happiness. If he had taken me to the donut shop that Noe and I always went to, I would have known that it had been more than just a coincidence, but this shop was different. We couldn't go inside to watch them make the donuts, but instead, had to stand outside of a giant glass window to watch. They hadn't opened the doors for business yet, so we had to stand outside, as though at an aquarium for human bakers.

When we had exited the taxi that Peter had gotten for us, I hadn't dared to say a word when I saw where we had stopped. Speaking of Noe and donuts and the significance of the two would have been too much for me to handle. Crying two times in one night was already too much. A third time would have completely broken me, even if the tears for the donut shop would have been happy tears. Together, we approached the window, since we saw that the sign on the door indicated that they did not open for another fifteen minutes, and watched the bakers work. The bakers inside, a lovely bunch of men and women, waved to us, indicating that they would be open soon, then went back to work. My eyes danced as I watched the bakers forming donuts out of dough, slipping them into the hot oil, and pulling out fresh, warm, brown dough that would be rolled in sugars, covered in icing, or filled with jelly or cremes. Peter laid a hand on my shoulder, giving it a squeeze as I watched the bakers and their seemingly choreographed dance around the shop kitchen.

It's an amazing thing, watching a group of employees at a business who seem to know each other as a family. They sense when someone is behind them, or that someone needs their help, they move and coordinate their efforts to be in sync with their counterparts without even looking. Although I couldn't hear the workers through the window of the kitchen, I didn't see them speaking much. So, I was amazed that even in their hurry to get the donuts ready for their first customers, they never bumped into each other or dropped anything. It was like a ballet that the bakers were performing, but with hot dough and cooking oil, and at a much faster pace. The fact that all of the shop's employees were smiling while they performed their work made everything all the more magical and enticing.

"Donuts make everyone happy," Peter said as he squeezed my shoulder.

"Donuts are the best." I agreed.

"Remember when I told you about the donuts at the shop where I'm from?" He asked in what was nearly a whisper. "The ones covered in powdered sugar and full of jam?"

"Yes?"

"I want to see if the ones they make here are better." He said. "We might have to eat quite a few just to be sure."

There was nothing to do but chuckle at that.

"I also did something horrible," Peter said.

Turning my eyes from the display in the donut shop was difficult, but I managed to do so. Peter saying that he had done something horrible got my attention immediately since I knew in my heart that the handsome American next to me had never done anything horrible in his life. Maybe a little bad, but never horrible.

"What did you do?" I asked, concern surely etched across my face.

"When you were praying earlier, uh, at the chapel?" He began.

"Yes?"

"I stepped outside, not just to smoke a cigarette, though that was part of it, but because I called a friend of mine here in Montreal."

"Oh?" I shrugged. "That is not horrible."

"I asked him if there were any jobs available at his office because I knew someone who needed one, and—"

"Peter."

"I know, I know." He grimaced. "I should have asked you first, Enzo. But he said he is looking for some office assistants, and, well, he said since I'm recommending you that if you want one of the positions, it's yours."

"Is this serious?"

"Again, I'm sorry, Enzo." Peter held his hands up defensively as I turned my body to look at him. "I should have asked, but watching you kneel there and pray, and knowing what little I knew about you already, I had to help if I could. Like...*real* help. Not just dinner and an ear."

"Well, yes, you should have asked." I couldn't make my eyes move to Peter's face.

It wasn't that I was upset that he had done such a thing without asking, or that he had done something that might have equated to pity. It was that I didn't know what to say to such a thoughtful gesture. The fact that I was suddenly faced with a solution to my biggest problem made it difficult to sort my thoughts as well.

"I hope you're not upset with me."

"No."

"I didn't mean to if I did."

"I'm not upset." I had to force myself to look up and meet his eyes.

"Are you sure?"

"Yes." I nodded. "I...I really need a job. Thank you."

Peter smiled at me suddenly, the worry that had darkened his face chased away by the brilliant flashing of teeth and crinkling at the edges of his eyes.

"So, I did a good thing?"

"Yes. You did a good thing." I reached out and nudged his shoulder with a smile. "It was very nice of you. I just...I don't know what to say. I am overwhelmed."

"You don't need to say anything." Peter shook his head furiously. "I don't need thanks or anything. I just want you to say that if I give you his number, you will call him tomorrow. He'll be waiting for your call if you do."

"Of course, I will call him." I agreed.

"Good." Peter's smile stretched further. "I'll give you his number. He said you could start immediately."

I felt my eyes threaten to tear up again, but I blinked a few times, refusing to cry over something so wonderful. Too many tears had been shed for far too long. For once, I wanted to just smile. So, I did.

"Okay."

Peter waved his hands erratically. "But, let's focus on donuts now. I just needed to tell you about that so it wasn't the last thing that I said to you after a wonderful night together. Okay?"

"Okay." I nodded, trying to push the thought of my financial problem being solved so easily out of my head.

"So," Peter turned back to the window, and I followed his lead. "Which donut are you going to try first?"

"Chocolate," I said. "Anything with chocolate."

Peter moaned with pleasure. "With crème filling, please."

"Yes." I moaned along.

We both laughed at the perverse sounds coming from our throats as one of the shop employees came to the front door, saw us, smiled brightly, and flipped the sign so that it read "OPEN." Peter gave me a nudge and a wink, and together, we strolled to the front door. The interior of the shop was warm and smelled of sugar, heavenly combinations. At the counter, Peter ordered six different types of donuts, and I followed his lead, asking for a duplicate order. Peter insisted on paying, and the cheerful shop employee accepted his payment while another employee filled a box with the donuts we had requested.

Instead of leaving the shop and finding another park in which to eat our treats, Peter led us to one of the small tables in the corner of the empty shop. Luckily, the tables were far enough away from the counter and the workers who were still busily making donuts, for us to have a conversation without fear of being overheard. Unbuttoning my coat, since the shop was sufficiently heated, I draped it carefully over the back of my chair and sat down. Peter slid into his seat across from me, placing the box full of donuts between us on the table. Peter mimicked my actions, though he had waited until he was seated to remove his gorgeous new coat. Finally, with both of our sleeves rolled up and our coats safe from powdered sugar, Peter flipped back the top of the box.

"Which one first?" He asked, peering into the box mischievously.

I shrugged. "The powdered sugar? It is the one you said you wanted to test the most."

"Powdered sugar it is." He winked at me from across the table.

In unison, we reached into the box, our fingers touching briefly before they found purchase around the sugary confection. Both of us gave satisfied moans—though much more quietly than we had outside—as we bit into the light, sugar-covered dough. Peter pulled the donut away from his mouth, his lips covered in powdered sugar, which made me laugh.

"What?"

I chewed my bite and swallowed quickly so I could answer.

"You have sugar all over your lips."

He leaned in. "Did you want to lick it off, or…"

Blushing, I looked away.

"Stop it."

"Do you really want me to stop?"

"Well, no."

"I didn't think so." He chuckled warmly and took another bite of his donut. "Is there anything better than warm, fresh donuts, Enzo? I mean, honestly? Other than obvious things like money and people, what else is this amazing?"

"I don't know."

"Well, I mean, sex is obviously better."

"I wouldn't know."

"How many times do I have to tell you?" Peter wiggled his eyebrows at me as the donut went to his mouth again, which he bit into and chewed before speaking again. "Everyone *knows* how good sex is, even if they've never had it."

"What if they don't like sex?" I countered.

"Like asexual people?"

I shrugged.

"Well, I'm talking about people who don't have an aversion."

"What if they do not have an aversion, but they are having sex with the wrong person?"

"You are thinking about this way too much."

"Sorry."

"It's okay." Peter winked. "At least I got you to admit you think about sex a lot."

"I did not!" I laughed, my face heating up.

"Yes, you did."

"You lie."

"Do I?" Peter teased as he stuffed the rest of the donut in his mouth. "Or do you not want to admit that you think about sex a lot?"

"I admitted nothing." I was still laughing, though mostly from nervousness.

"But do you?" Peter reached into the box and grabbed another donut. "Think of sex?"

The chocolate one.

It looked delicious.

"Why are you doing this to me?" I groaned as I reached for my chocolate donut.

Though I never would have admitted it to Peter, I didn't want him to stop talking to me about sex. I didn't necessarily want him to become graphic with his talk, but speaking of sex in general terms was very pleasing and arousing. Eating delicious, sugary donuts and having a handsome man to talk about sex with at the same time was definitely not the worst way to spend one's time. The fact that Peter was so easy to talk to, though I was still embarrassed, made it all better. Peter wouldn't do anything to shame me or humiliate me, no matter what we talked about. I felt safe discussing anything with him.

"Because I enjoy talking with you about sex."

"Why?"

"Really?" Peter rolled his eyes. "Have you seen yourself, Enzo? I think anyone would enjoy talking about sex with you."

Blushing was all I could do in response, so I shoved nearly half of the chocolate donut in my mouth to try and distract my mind.

"Do you like talking about sex with me?"

"This is too much," I said, my mouth stuffed with dough and chocolate.

"Really?"

"Yes. But in a good way."

"Good." Peter grinned happily and took another bite of his donut.

Swallowing the donut down, I made sure my eyes met Peter's.

"Is this how you think you will make me happy?" I asked. "Donuts and talking about sex?"

"Is it working?"

"Well…yes."

"Distracting, isn't it?" He shrugged. "Sugar and sex can always make people forget their problems, at least for a little bit."

"But what happens to your problems once the sugar is gone and the sex is over?"

"You get more sugar and have more sex." He winked.

"Have?" I found the courage to grin back. "I thought this was just talking?"

Peter held a hand to his chest dramatically.

"Gosh." He groaned. "Right in the heart."

I laughed.

"So, do you think about sex a lot?" He reiterated, stuffing the last of his chocolate donut in his mouth.

"You will not stop until I answer this question, will you?"

"Probably not," He said. "I'm very stubborn."

"I mean…I don't think so?" I knew that I may as well answer the question because Peter would not give up. And I wanted to answer him. "Not really, I do not think."

"What's that mean?" Peter was reaching for another donut.

I loved that he loved to eat, and he was not afraid for me to know it.

"I think that when I think of sex, it is not really about sex," I said, reaching for another donut as well. "I have never really met anyone that I thought of...*like that*...so when I think of sex, it is..."

"Vague?"

"Yes."

"So," Peter glanced towards the counter, then leaned in, "what do you think of when you masturbate?"

"Peter!" I laughed sharply, my face immediately turning hot.

"What?" Peter grinned. "Everyone does it."

"Well, yes. But—"

"Don't be shy, Enzo."

"I am not shy."

"The red on your cheeks says otherwise. And you are far too pale for it to not be noticeable."

"What do you think about?" I countered.

Peter took a bite of his donut, much daintier than with the first two donuts.

"Usually hot guys that I've seen." He said. "Either in person or like movie stars and stuff. Sometimes I watch porn."

"Zut."

"I'm sorry?"

"Uh...*damn*."

Peter grinned. "Do you watch porn, Enzo?"

"On what?" I snorted. "The huge television in my living room?"

Peter laughed nervously.

"I am just being silly," I said.

"Okay. I hope I didn't offend you."

"You did not offend me," I said. "But no. I do not watch...*porn*."

I whispered the last word.

"Then, what do you think about?" He asked before biting into his donut.

"Peter."

"Oh, come on." He said. "When we have our second date, I will need to know these things."

"You think you will need to know about this on our second date?"

"No." He smiled. "I just wanted to hear you say there would be a second date."

"You are awful."

"You love it."

I looked down, overcome with bravado by the conversation over a box of delicious, fresh, warm donuts.

"I love spending time with you," I said. "Even though you are awful."

"I love spending time with you, too," Peter replied. "Even though you are not awful."

"I think about having someone…like you…who makes me feel safe." I said, looking down. "Who will make me feel comfortable having…sex. When I…do that."

When I looked up, Peter was smiling.

"If that was your attempt at being awful, you failed." He said. "And I've never been so happy to see someone fail."

"I am very sad suddenly."

"Why?" He frowned.

"I do not want you to leave."

"I don't want to leave either."

In unison, we reached into the box, each of us grabbing our fourth donut. Both of us grabbed a chocolate donut filled with crème, meant to look like an éclair but not quite achieving the goal. It looked delicious either way.

"Enzo?"

"Yes?" I bit into the donut.

It was just as good as an actual éclair, though I would have felt bad for saying so out loud to anyone but Peter.

"Would you ever come visit me in America?" He asked. "If you were able?"

"I have never been to America."

"That's not the question."

I smiled. "Would you like it if I visited you?"

"Yes." He sighed dreamily. "I would love to have you come visit me. I would like for you to come visit as often as you like. You could…"

"What?" I had learned to not wait with Peter.

"You could stay as long as you want."

"That is ridiculous."

"I know." He shrugged. "I don't care."

"So, you do not want a second date?" I teased. "You want to be my boyfriend."

Peter couldn't contain his laughter. "That is so juvenile. I love it."

"I do not know what else to call it."

"Partner." He said. "Maybe you could be my partner."

"And make your house my castle?" I continued the thought. "And we will wake up on Sundays and kiss and have breakfast and…be not so sweet…and walk to the market, then make dinner, and feed scraps to our dog?"

"And then be not so sweet again before falling asleep in each other's arms." He nodded. "Are you happy right now?"

"Yes."

"Mission accomplished." He said. "Imagine how happy you would be if you visited me in America."

"What would your family think? Your friends?"

"They know I'm gay."

I frowned. "I mean…I am…you are…"

"I'm old, and you aren't?" He teased.

"Well, yes. I suppose?"

"I don't know." He replied. "My last boyfriend was more age-appropriate, I guess. They might be shocked at first, but they would get used to it. Especially after they saw how wonderful you are, anyway."

"What if they didn't like me?"

"Then they could fuck off."

I laughed and stuffed more of the donut into my mouth.

"Enzo." Peter sighed and sat back, ignoring his last two donuts. "I know I'm a fool. But I like you. And I don't want you to think that I am just saying this stuff so I can simply have a fun night. I truly like you. I want to be able to like you for many more nights after tonight."

"I truly like you, too, Peter."

"So…will you promise me something?"

"I will try."

"If the time comes that you are able to come to America to visit, you will do it, right? I can send you a plane ticket, or—"

"I will come to America to visit." I nodded, cutting him off. "But only if I can buy my own plane ticket. You have been kind tonight. And I have allowed it. But if we are to be partners, I do not want you to be…I do not want to be taken care of by anyone."

"You want to want to be there. You don't want to need me."

"Yes. Exactly."

"Deal." He smiled. "Then I will give you my friend's phone number. Take the job. Work. Get your life in order. And as soon as you have the money, you have to come see me."

"Will you expect me to have sex with you?"

Peter coughed, nearly choking on his donut.

"Why would you think that?" He asked, his eyes wide. "I wouldn't expect you to do anything you didn't want to do, Enzo."

"Oh?" I grinned. "I would expect it of you."

Peter's horrified expression slowly turned into a wicked grin.

"Ah." He said. "You were asking if this will be romantic in nature and if it might lead to sex?"

"Yes."

"Absolutely." Peter reached over and thumped me on the end of my nose. "I am not asking you to come to America just to be friends. Though your friendship is important, too."

"May I ask you one last favor, Peter?"

"Anything."

"When it is time for you to leave today, do not look back." I sighed. "I do not want to see your eyes as you are walking away."

"What if I want to see yours one last time?"

"That would mean you expect to never see them again."

Peter stared at me for the longest of moments.

"Okay," Peter said. "I won't look back. As long as you promise I will see your eyes again."

"I promise."

Peter sat back in his chair, and I sat back in mine, our eyes locked. We each had two donuts left. Slowly, Peter started to put his coat back on, slipping his arms inside of it as I mimicked his actions. We were both fools. Two strangers who met by chance and struck up a romance in less time than some people sleep in a night. But in my heart of hearts, as we put on our coats across the table from each other, I knew that I would go see Peter in America one day. What happened after that, I wasn't sure, but I would never be truly happy again unless I found out.

"Why don't we go watch the sunrise and eat the rest of our donuts?" Peter suggested, leaning in to smile at me.

"Okay."

How One Comes to Own a Coat

Noe wasn't sudden or drawn out. He was both. His breathing got worse between Christmas and New Year's, and then we started spending a lot of time at the doctors' offices and A&E. It was rare that a week would go by that we were not at one or the other. Noe's medical conditions were nothing new to us, though we both knew that he was having trouble overcoming his recent bout with his chronic obstructive pulmonary disease. His asthma flared up nearly every day. It was hard to get to work on time and perform all of my duties for an entire shift because Noe needed me more and more as the days went by. This went on for months until we were barely able to pay rent and also afford a sufficient amount of food to keep us decently fed. In fact, many days, I rationed out my calories so that I could be sure that Noe was getting enough to eat, though his appetite decreased with each passing day.

At the end of summer, Noe had to be admitted to the hospital. So, we were both sleeping in his hospital room every night as machines "beeped" and "booped" and nurses came in to check on him periodically, always waking both of us. I took showers in his hospital bathroom and went home to change clothes before going to work. Then I would be back at the hospital to repeat the entire process of barely getting any rest before starting another day. Noe was restless every night due to the medicines they gave him and the nurses bothering us throughout the night. The hospital bed was not the bed he was used to, and he said the sheets and blankets were "scratchy."

Regardless of the strain we were under, Noe slowly started to get better over the days he spent in the hospital. The doctors, for once, seemed very caring and attentive, cheerful, and optimistic about Noe's prognosis. They said that it would take time in the hospital for Noe to get better so that he could go home, but they didn't doubt that he would, in fact, get better. On our final night in the hospital, a nurse had come in before bedtime to let us know that Noe would most likely be discharged the following afternoon. Noe gave his version of a smile when the news was delivered, and I felt nothing less than relief and joy.

The following morning, after the two of us woke up and had breakfast, and I had taken a shower, I held Noe's forearm and told him that I was going to go home and get him some fresh clothes and his coat. It was still summer, but I knew having his coat made of sugar and blue clouds would make him feel better on our way home. Noe told me to hurry because he wanted to leave as soon as the doctors said he could. He had grown as weary of the hospital as I had.

So, I went home and took another shower, wanting to be as clean and feel as fresh as I could for bringing Noe home. I gathered up a bag of his clothes and draped his blue coat over my shoulder. Then I walked the few kilometers back to the hospital.

An embolism. So, it was sudden, Noe's death. But it was the end to months of health problems that all of the doctors seemed to think could be resolved.

When I left the hospital that morning, Noe was fine. We were going to go home and be our own little family again. When I went back to the hospital, my brother was gone. It happened so suddenly and so quickly, there hadn't even been time to call me. They had been trying to save Noe's life instead.

I sat in a hospital room with what was once my brother, his forearm in one of my hands and the coat made of sugar and blue clouds in my other.

The universe had dealt a final blow. Nothing else could be taken from me.

Or, that's what I thought. Until a blue coat was stolen from a hook in a classroom over a dumpling restaurant.

Between the Universe and Me

Peter and I sat in St. Louis Square again after another short taxi ride. Now that the sun was getting closer to rising, sitting on the ledge of the fountain with all of the gorgeous houses surrounding us didn't seem so dangerous. If someone were to come along and asked us why we were sitting at the fountain at such an hour, we would have the excuse of wanting to watch the sunrise. We would have had no excuse hours earlier. Our donut box was on the fountain ledge between us, open and empty. We had moved quickly to finish our donuts upon arriving at the square. Due to the approaching dawn and thoughts of Peter having to leave for America, neither of us spoke much. What could be said about something unavoidable? All we could do was enjoy each other's company, eat our donuts, and watch the sunrise.

As I sat there, a fairly small white cardboard box the only thing separating us, I didn't think about my problems or sorrows. My family and what had become of it, the awful people in my ESL class, Noe's stolen coat, the rude food vendor in the market—all of it was a distant memory, at least for the time being. The Lazy Duck, the park, the square, the donuts, the M&Ms and Smarties, the taxi rides, the flirtation…Peter having to leave…that was all I thought of and cared about as we waited for the sun to peek over the horizon. Overnight, it had gotten even colder in the city, but somehow, with the threat of dawn, the wind was still, and the city seemed warmer. It was if everything was waiting for the sun's warm rays to bathe every surface in golden light and start the day anew. I've always loved the mornings, especially before the sun rises. A new day is a new start, and if you beat the sun in waking up, you can feel the anticipation and hope of its imminent arrival. Nothing fills me with hope like waiting for the sun to arrive, dragging the new day behind it.

Beside me, with that cardboard barrier between us, Peter sat silently, looking easterly towards the row of houses that the sun would peek over once it arrived. Without asking, I knew that he felt the same way that I did. While our night together, which we decided to declare our first date, hadn't been all smiles and fun, it had been extraordinary. Both of us had spent the night with someone who understood them deeply, who wanted the other person to feel loved and cared for, without judgment or expectation. Two people met by chance—or maybe they found each other on purpose—and decided to listen to the universe's suggestion. It would have been just as easy for either of us to have walked away at the autumn festival, to decide that there was no point in talking to a stranger with the expectation that they might be the very person we needed most that night. Peter and I had decided to do the opposite of what came so naturally to both of us.

My life had never been a series of logical events that were leading up to something greater. It had always seemed that with each great thing, my life got more difficult, sadder, more overwhelming. I wasn't sure as I sat there on the ledge of the fountain why I had allowed Peter to walk into my life when good things always seemed to herald doom. Maybe a handsome red-haired American was too irresistible. Maybe I was tired of expecting doom every time something good happened. Or maybe, somehow, I had decided to trust the universe again.

No. I didn't trust the universe.

Not because I thought it didn't care about me, but because it had too many people to care about.

I was just Enzo.

I was one of billions—if not trillions—of concerns the universe had to deal with each day. So, the universe did not have my trust simply because I knew the universe wouldn't know if I trusted it anyway.

As we sat there, the sky growing lighter, and the neighborhood around us beginning to become bathed in a pale violet-y blue color, I wondered about kismet. That was how Peter described our meeting. Had all of my prayers finally been heard…or had a series of events just coincidentally placed us in each other's path? Was there a difference? What are prayers but a wish for your hopes and dreams to be manifested in some way? The method doesn't really matter, one just hopes that someone is listening and gently guides them towards bringing those thoughts to fruition. A person could call that *thing* God or providence or the universe, but it was really all the same thing. Prayers send out thoughts, and we hope for the best. For one night in my life, I had gotten the best.

"I've never been so unhappy thinking about a sunrise before." Peter sighed.

"Me either."

"Maybe if I knew how long I'd have to wait to see you again after today, it wouldn't feel so awful."

On our way to the square in the taxi, Peter had taken my mobile phone and entered his phone number and the phone number of his friend who had a job waiting for me. The wait to see each other again did not have to be long. It all rested on how well the job paid. There was only one way to find that out.

"It will not be too long," I said.

"I hope not."

"Do you think I will like America?"

"I'll be there. Why wouldn't you?"

I chuckled, still unable to pry my eyes from the houses in the east so that I could look into Peter's eyes. Looking at him would make the fact that he was leaving all too real. I didn't want him to leave, and I didn't want to think about what it meant to be so sad to see a stranger leave.

"Of course, I will be happy you are there," I said gently. "But tell me what else I will love."

In the corner of my eye, I could see Peter turn his head to look at me.

"Well, there's the food." He began. "Like Montreal, you can find all kinds of food in Minneapolis. It's a pretty diverse city. It's very friendly to the LGBTQ community. So, we could kiss in the middle of town, and no one would care. Usually. There are movie theaters and museums. Parks. It's not far from the Great Lakes if we wanted to take a weekend trip. My parents only live an hour away…if you wanted to meet them. I have a lot of friends who would love you and treat you like they've known you their entire lives. It's really nice. And I'll be there."

"That is my favorite part."

"I think I will like Minneapolis even more if you are there."

The first rays of the sun began to peek over the tops of the houses. The violet-blue of the neighborhood slowly began to turn gold.

"Here comes the sun," I said.

"I love that song." Peter chuckled.

"What?"

"The Beatles?" He said. "It's a song by them. *Here Comes the Sun.*"

"I have never heard it."

Peter didn't say anything more, he simply pulled his fancy phone from his pocket and tapped the screen for a few moments as the neighborhood and square slowly became more golden. Suddenly, nearly making me jump, music started to play softly from Peter's phone. After the first few chords, I couldn't help but smile as I watched the sun climb over the tops of the houses. As the seconds went by, and the song played, and the sun climbed higher, starting to peek over the rooves of the houses, I unbuttoned my new coat and slid it off of my shoulders, then neatly laid it along the ledge of the fountain. I stood and took a few steps away from the fountain, greeting the sun and the brand-new day, a smile coming to my face as the warmth of our closest star licked at my flesh. The Beatles sang their lullaby as my eyes drooped shut, and I smiled at the warmth on my face.

A moment later, I heard the music getting closer, then suddenly I sensed Peter in front of me.

"I'm going to kiss you now." He said lowly. "And then I'm going to leave. Okay?"

"Okay," I said, keeping my eyes shut, though my smile never faltered.

"And I won't look back."

"Okay."

Bracing myself, I felt Peter step into the beam of sun that had been warming my face. My whole body seemed to be a live wire of nerves, anticipating the kiss, and also dreading it. What if I did something wrong? What if he kissed me and suddenly felt differently? I had been rejected many times before, but I had never been rejected as a sexual being. I wasn't sure I could handle such a thing, having no experience with it. My instincts told me to step back, to pull away, do anything but let his lips touch mine. Another part of me told my instincts to shut the fuck up because I wanted nothing more than to know what Peter's lips tasted like. So, I forced myself to stand still, my eyes closed, as Peter moved closer.

Peter's hand was against my chest, laying there for a moment before it traveled upward, to the flesh of my throat, around to the side of my neck, and then up the back of my neck so that his fingers could get tangled in the short hairs there. I felt the warmth of his body move up against mine as he moved his face closer. I desperately wanted to know if his eyes were also closed like I'd seen people do when kissing in movies or other couples did in public. Did he have his eyes open, not wanting to miss the look on my face when I received my first kiss? In the end, I knew that I could not bear to open my eyes and see Peter's, knowing it would be the last time that

I would see them. I would have to make do with the kiss being my last sensation of being with him. For now.

Then I felt Peter pull gently against my head as he moved his face toward mine. My whole body threatened to collapse, as though I was going to let out a breath I hadn't known I'd been holding, making me deflate until I was a puddle on the ground. Somehow, I managed to keep my knees locked and stay on my feet as Peter's lips finally pressed against mine. Gently at first, testing how his lips felt against mine. Then more firmly, as though suddenly infatuated with what they felt, trying to devour me and memorize that feeling. My hands rose to Peter's hips, gently laying against them as his fingers tightened in my hair, and his lips memorized mine.

I knew that the kiss lasted long enough that anyone passing by might have been scandalized, but it never could have lasted long enough to satisfy me. With the first feel of Peter's lips, the taste of him coursing over my mouth, I never wanted it to end. The strength with which Peter held onto me, the way his fingers tangled in my hair, I knew he was fighting his own battle. But finally, as all things go, I felt him pull back just far enough to sigh, his breath warm against my face. Bit by bit, his fingers loosened in my hair, and his hand slid from the back of my head, back around my neck, over my throat, and down to my chest. For a moment, he let his hand lay there again as I stood before him, eyes still shut, afraid to look at him.

"Whenever you get to America," He whispered, his mouth still dangerously close to mine, "it won't be soon enough, Enzo. I'll miss you."

"I will miss you, too," I whispered back, my lips fluttering against his.

Without another word, I felt Peter's hand reluctantly pull away from my chest, and his body move away. The music stopped. I wanted to open my eyes to see if he was struggling to walk away from me. I wanted to know that leaving Montreal—leaving me—was one of the hardest things he ever had to do.

"This is only 'goodbye' for now." He said firmly, his voice further away.

"Okay."

"Goodbye, for now, Enzo."

"Goodbye, for now, Peter." It nearly came out like a sob, but my happiness overruled it.

When I finally was able to open my eyes, though I was unsure how long I waited, Peter was nowhere in sight. It was almost as if he had never existed at all, though I knew that was just my mind playing tricks on me, trying to convince me that something so wonderful couldn't have been true. When a person goes for too long without goodness in their lives, it seems unlikely when it arrives, and like a fantasy when it is gone again. Standing in the middle of the square with the now golden neighborhood bearing down on me, I couldn't bear to stay still. So, I went to the fountain and got my coat—my new coat that Peter had so selflessly given to me—and slipped it back on.

Shoving my hands into the warm lined pockets of my new coat, I forced myself to take in the houses bathed in gold around the square and smile. Even if Peter was gone, and even if I never saw him again, at least I had experienced one of the greatest nights of my life and my first kiss. Even if there had been tears and sadness, there had also been joy and healing. Peter had helped me to understand that even after death, there is life. There is no greater gift one can receive than that. Somehow, I knew that things would get better between the universe and me. For all of my trying, all of my struggles, I knew that I was not perfect. I hadn't been the best grandson, son, or brother. But I had done my best. Maybe the universe was just doing the best it could, too.

I found myself walking along Ave des Pins E after leaving the square, wondering where life would take me next. Calling Peter's friend would be my first task the following day. And it would be my life's mission to visit Peter in America, no matter how long that took, but in the meantime, I had no idea what life had in store for me. I was okay with that. Once a

313

person is sure that life can have good things waiting ahead, it makes it easier to put one foot in front of the other, to keep moving forward until the good times arrive. The smile would not leave my face as I turned onto St. Urbain Street, heading in the direction of my apartment once again.

Where was Peter in Montreal? Was he already back at his hotel, packing for his flight home, after hailing a taxi somewhere in the city? Was he thinking of me as much as I was thinking of him? Was the thought of getting on a plane to leave Montreal as hard on him as it was on me? I didn't want Peter to feel remorse or sadness in leaving the city, but I wouldn't have minded knowing that it was not easy for him, either. I would have given anything to know that he would miss me until the moment I stepped off of a plane in Minneapolis sometime in the future. And I hoped that as soon as he saw me step off of the plane, that sadness would melt away immediately. I wanted to see the light return to his eyes the first time I saw them after closing mine by the fountain in the square.

Maybe I was foolish and ridiculous. Maybe I was acting as though I was a character in a fairytale. Sometimes, all you can do is pretend that life is a fairytale just so you can get through one moment to the next. With Peter on my mind, I knew that the following days would be much warmer. Much easier. As I passed the dumpling restaurant that had Mr.

Paquette's classroom above it, I stopped and stared at the building. A smile immediately came to my face. If it hadn't been for Mr. Paquette insisting that I go get something to eat...if it hadn't been for someone stealing Noe's coat...I never would have met Peter. There was no way that the universe had not had a hand in orchestrating those events.

When my eyes caught a flash of sky-blue fabric hanging from the doorknob of the restaurant, my breath caught in my throat. Jerkily, I stumbled towards the building, nearly drunk with disbelief as I approached the door. Getting closer, I realized it was Noe's coat. A simple scrap of white paper was paperclipped to the sleeve. *"This is Enzo's. Sorry."*

I suppose the universe finally said the one word I had needed it to say.

The End.

About the Author

Chase Connor currently lives in Des Moines, Iowa with his dog, Rimbaud, and spends his free time writing M/M Romance, LGBTQ YA novellas/novels, LGBTQ Paranormal Romance, as well as general LGBTQ fiction, when he's not busy being enthusiastic about naps and Pad Thai.

Chase can be reached at
chaseconnor@chaseconnor.com
Or on Twitter @ChaseConnor7
He can also be found on Chase Connor Books
https://chaseconnor.com
(New blog posts every Tuesday)

He does his very best to respond to all DMs, emails, and Twitter comments from his reader friends and loves the interaction with them. Chase has several novellas/novels for sale on Amazon (and other sites) in ebook and paperback format.

Most of Chase Connor's catalog can be read for FREE on Kindle Unlimited

Lightning Source UK Ltd.
Milton Keynes UK
UKHW012016150120
357039UK00001B/30/P